"I'm starting an art foundation, and I'm looking for artists to sponsor and a gallery to exhibit their work. I think Vogel's might be perfect."

For a second, she thought she must have misheard him. But at the same time she knew she hadn't. Joy burst inside her. Vogel's was saved! She wanted to kiss Garek Wisnewski right on the mouth….

Almost as if he could read her mind, his gaze dropped to her lips.

Her mental celebrations came to a screeching halt. He'd looked at her mouth that way in his office. Right before he'd told her to contact him if she wanted to "offer" him something.

She leaned back in her seat, her smile fading. What was going on here? What was the catch?

Judging from the way he was looking at her mouth, she suspected she knew exactly what the catch was.

A RITA® Award-winning author for her first novel, **Angie Ray** has written historical and paranormal novels, but this is her first category romance. The mind of this native Southern Californian is buzzing with ideas for stories, and she loves brainstorming while taking walks. Her husband and two children also provide plenty of distraction, but sooner or later she's always drawn back to her computer for 'just one more scene'—which invariably leads to another book!

THE MILLIONAIRE'S REWARD

BY
ANGIE RAY

MILLS & BOON®

First published in Great Britain 2006
Harlequin Mills & Boon Limited,
Eton House, 18-24 Paradise Road, Richmond, Surrey TW9 1SR

© Angela Ray 2005

ISBN-13: 978 0 263 84871 7
ISBN-10:   0 263 84871 X

Set in Times Roman 10½ on 12¼ pt
01-1206-44043

Printed and bound in Spain
by Litografia Rosés, S.A., Barcelona

THE MILLIONAIRE'S REWARD

Chapter One

The necklace was the gaudiest, ugliest piece of jewelry Garek Wisnewski had ever seen.

Rubies and emeralds vied for glittering supremacy in a bright yellow-gold setting decorated with enough curlicues and whorls to make a Russian czar blink. Any woman wearing this necklace risked blinding innocent bystanders—or being mistaken for a Christmas tree. This bauble had nothing to do with beauty or elegance—it was about money, pure and simple.

"It's perfect," he told the chignoned blonde behind the counter who'd been batting her eyelashes at him ever since he entered the store. "I'll take it."

"An excellent choice," she congratulated him. "You have exquisite taste, Mr. Wisnewski."

"Thank you."

The young woman didn't appear to notice the irony in his voice. Placing the necklace in a satin-lined case and ringing up the sale, she chatted vivaciously. "Women adore rubies and emeralds. They're so much more interesting than diamonds, don't you think? I'm sure your girlfriend will love the necklace."

She paused to check his reaction to her comment, and he recognized the look in her eyes. In the last hellish month, he'd been forced to deal with numerous women, all with similar predatory expressions. He'd devised several strategies to deal with them: attack, retreat and play dead.

He used the attack method only in extreme situations; the blond salesclerk didn't qualify—at least not yet. Retreat was impossible until he got his credit card back. Which left only one option.

He didn't offer either a confirmation or a denial of her guess about the necklace's recipient.

She wasn't deterred by his lack of response, however. Finishing the transaction, she slid the jewelry case across the glass counter—along with a business card.

"My home phone number's on the back. If you ever want a private viewing of our…inventory, please call me."

Garek shoved the box into his pocket, but left the card on the counter. "That won't be necessary," he growled.

He strode to the door, almost bumping into another customer who blew into the shop, along with a freezing gust of wind. Short and round, the man stood in the doorway, nose dripping, as he stared up at Garek.

"Hey, I know you!" The man's Neanderthal forehead cleared and he winked at Garek. "I saw your picture in the *Chicago Trumpeter* this morning. Hank, right? Heh, heh, heh—"

"Excuse me," Garek said icily. "You're blocking the door."

The man stopped sniggering and quickly stepped aside. Garek exited, shutting the shop door with a bang. He stood on the cold, dark sidewalk, sleet stinging his face and hands.

He yanked on his gloves and wrapped his muffler around the lower half of his face. Annoyance making his steps brisker than usual, he headed down the sidewalk, cursing himself for ever agreeing to talk to that damn reporter.

He'd broken his usual no-interview rule because she'd said she was doing an article on how business-men had contributed to the revitalization of the city by providing jobs for displaced workers. If he'd known what she really intended, he would have shown her out of his office immediately. Now, because of lowering his guard for one moment, his life had become a liv-ing hell. Oh, he'd been mildly amused at first. The rib-ald jokes from the men. The fluttering glances from the women. But then, he'd started getting letters. Sacks of them. And women started showing up at his office. And his apartment. At restaurants where he was dining…

Lengthening his stride, he stepped over a puddle. Last night had been the final straw. He'd been about to close a deal with a prospective client over smoked pork tenderloin and Yukon Gold mashed potatoes when an enterprising young woman named Lilly Lade had shown up professing to be a singing-telegram girl—but she'd seemed more interested in stripping than singing. While horrified matrons looked on, he'd had to bun-dle the woman up and forcibly escort her from the restaurant.

Unfortunately, once outside, she'd thrown her arms

around his neck and planted a kiss on his mouth. He'd thrust Lilly away, but not before a tabloid photographer had snapped several shots.

Trying to ignore the freezing wind, Garek hunched his shoulders and turned the corner to where his limousine waited. The situation was no longer amusing. In fact, he was damn well fed up—

"Oof!"

A woman made the small sound as she ran into him at full speed. The packages in her arms went flying. And so did she. She landed on her rear in the snow.

Instinctively, he crouched by her side. "Are you all right?"

Her blue eyes, framed by long black lashes, looked slightly dazed, but she nodded. "I'm fine...."

His gaze dropped to her mouth, watching her lips form the words. Her upper lip was long and perfectly straight, with no indentation at all, curling up slightly at the corners. The lower lip was shorter, and fuller, but not much. The effect was amazingly sensual.

He bent closer to hear her over the whistling wind.

"I'm so sorry—"

"It was my fault," he interrupted, dragging his gaze away from her mouth. "I wasn't looking where I was going."

"No, no. I was running, trying to catch my train— oh, my things!"

With only slight support from his steadying arm, she scrambled to her feet and grabbed a box that had fallen onto the ground. A turquoise scarf and tissue paper peeping out from under the crushed lid, she stuffed the box back into her bag.

"Are you sure you're all right?" He picked up her hat

and she crammed it onto her head, the bright red yarn concealing all but a few short black curls.

"Yes, I'm sure." She smiled ruefully, her teeth very white against the golden hue of her skin, a dimple appearing in her cheek. "My packages have suffered the most, I think."

"Let me help you," he said, capturing a bag on the verge of blowing away. He swept several small boxes into it, his attention focused more on her than his task. She didn't seem to recognize him—a rarity these days. He couldn't see her figure, wrapped up as it was in a slightly shabby coat that was several sizes too big. But she was small, perhaps an inch or two over five feet, and he'd felt the fine bones of her hand through her mitten when he'd helped her up.

He picked up a tiny pair of pink, yellow and blue tennis shoes. He glanced at the woman again. Young—but not too young to have a child. "There's mud on these shoes. I'll replace them and anything else that's damaged."

"Oh, no!" she protested immediately. "It'll wash off. And if it doesn't, my niece won't notice a few spots… oh!"

She hurried off to retrieve a baseball rolling slowly down the gutter toward a storm drain. He saw a magazine, its pages fluttering in the wind. "Is this yours?" he called to her as he bent to pick it up.

She glanced over her shoulder and nodded, before reaching for the baseball.

Garek picked up the magazine, then froze as he saw his own face staring up at him from the cover.

His jaw tightened. Ramming the tabloid into the sack, he stalked over to where she crouched in the gutter. As she stood up, he shoved the bag into her arms.

"Here," he said curtly. "Watch where you're going next time."

He stomped away, only to step directly into a puddle. Icy water splashed into the top of his shoe. Cursing under his breath, he squelched down the street to the waiting limo and climbed inside. "Home, Hardeep."

"Yes, sir," the chauffeur replied.

The car purring down the street, Garek looked out the window. He saw the woman still standing in the gutter, clutching her bags and staring at the limo. She wore an expression of profound bewilderment.

Anger swept through him. She must have been lurking on the corner, waiting for him. If the magazine hadn't given her away, he would've believed their collision was an accident. He'd even been about to offer her a ride home.

Oh, she was good, better than most. Innocent-looking—except for her mouth. He should have been warned by that mouth....

He sat in brooding silence until the chauffeur stopped in front of his apartment building. Not until he went inside and reached into his pocket did he realize that something was missing.

The emerald-and-ruby necklace was gone.

Cold, wet and tired, Ellie entered her apartment and dumped her bags on the small kitchenette table with a sigh of relief. "Hi, Martina," she said to her cousin who was checking a large pot on the stove. "How'd you do on your final?"

"Fine. It was easier than I expected." Martina lifted a steamer, laden with tamales, from the pot and set them on the counter. She glanced over her shoulder, her long, dark hair swinging. Her already well-arched brows rose. "What happened to you, *chica?*"

Ellie shook her head as she pulled off her coat and wet mittens and walked over to hold her cold hands next to the ancient but blessedly warm furnace. "It's a long story. Suffice it to say I bumped into Mr. Grinch and missed my train." She sniffed the air appreciatively. "Those tamales smell awfully good. Can I have one?"

"Well…okay, but just one. They're for the party tomorrow night. Who's this Mr. Grinch?"

"Nobody," Ellie dismissed the unpleasant man. Although in truth, with his sleek leather gloves and expensive limo he'd obviously been *somebody*. Somebody rich and spoiled who'd suddenly decided she wasn't worth the time and effort it took to be polite. Sinking into a chair, she peeled back the hot corn husk and bit into the tamale. The spiced meat inside burned her mouth, but she was too hungry to care. "Mmm, this is fantastic, Martina. Better than your father's. You should sell these. You'd make a fortune."

"I like cooking…but not that much." Briskly, Martina piled the tamales into a glass dish. "How was business at the gallery today?"

"Not bad. A lot of people came in. I talked one couple into taking a painting home to try it out. And I sold a sculpture." Carefully, Ellie broke a piece off the tamale and watched a thin wisp of steam rise into the air. "The woman loved it. She said it reminded her of the feeling she had when she first fell in love. She didn't even look at the price tag. But when I told her how much it was, she said she couldn't afford that much, and could I please give her a discount. I told her maybe a small one, but she said she could only pay half the price and so—"

"And so you ended up practically giving it away," Martina finished for her, shaking her head. "You never could bargain worth a dime. A Hernandez without the haggle gene—it's unnatural."

Ellie made a face at her cousin. "I'm getting better."

"Yeah, right. I thought you said Mr. Vogel was going to have to close the gallery if it didn't start making a profit."

Ellie bit her lip. She *had* said that—and it was the truth. The thought scared her. She'd worked hard, but the gallery had failed to meet its expenses the last three months in a row. If she didn't figure something out soon, Mr. Vogel wouldn't be able to afford to keep it open. And then what would Tom and Bertrice and all the other artists who showed their works at the gallery do? What would *she* do? She loved her job.

Okay, so occasionally she had to clean houses on the side to make ends meet—what was a little drudgery when she had the gallery to look forward to? At Vogel's, a hundred exciting, unexpected things could happen. A sculptor could come in, eager to debate the merits of his latest creation. A scruffy college student could walk through the door, carrying a portfolio of the most amazing sketches she'd ever seen. Or a customer could come in, someone eager to escape their narrow existence and view the world through a different perspective—a perspective of shape and form and color....

"Sales will pick up," she told Martina with more confidence than she felt.

"You need to advertise. Business is all about advertising." Martina, majoring in marketing at a nearby college, considered herself—at age twenty-one—an expert in all things related to business. "And contacts. You need to cultivate the right people."

Ellie grimaced. "You mean suck up to some rich business executives and their spouses?"

"It's called networking. You're such a snob, Ellie."

"I am not!"

"When it comes to art, you are. My heart bleeds for that poor woman who came to the gallery yesterday—"

"Martina! I told you what she said—"

"Oh, yes, she wanted to know if the painting would be a good investment. It's not a crime, Ellie, to want to make money."

"If she wants to make money, she should invest in real estate." Ellie glanced over her shoulder at the worn leather sofa in the living room—and the multihued art-works that covered every square inch of the wall above. "Art shouldn't be about money."

Martina rolled her eyes. "You're missing the point, Ellie. It *is* about money—at least for now. You should have found something to sell that woman, not suggested she try another gallery. You need to think like a business-man." Martina put the tamales in the refrigerator, then approached the bags on the table. "Did you get my magazine?"

"Yes, it's in there somewhere." Ellie nibbled her tamale absently. Was Martina right? Was she a snob when it came to art? Maybe. Well, okay, probably. An artist poured so much of himself into a piece, spent so much time and effort to get the composition, the colors, the textures and a thousand other details just exactly right. It seemed wrong somehow to let someone who cared nothing about the artist's creative endeavor take a piece home.

Unfortunately, she couldn't worry about right and wrong anymore.

She swallowed a bite of tamale with difficulty. She

couldn't allow the gallery to close because she didn't like the fact that someone saw dollar signs instead of art when they looked at a painting. She couldn't afford to demand that people appreciate a painting or a sculpture the way it deserved to be appreciated. "Okay, Martina. From now on, I'll act like a businessman. I'll be cold, hard, ruthless—"

"Maybe you can just be practical…what's this?" Martina let out a low whistle.

Ellie glanced up to see her cousin staring down at the contents of a flat jeweler's box.

"What'd you do, Ellie? Make a withdrawal at the bank?"

Brushing the soft *masa* crumbs off her fingers, Ellie got up to look in the box. She gasped when she saw its contents.

Emeralds and rubies flashed in the apartment's dim light, their sparkle silent testimony to their authenticity.

"Good heavens," Ellie said faintly. "It must belong to that man—Mr. Grinch."

"He's not going to be happy when he finds it missing," Martina observed.

"No, I don't think so," Ellie agreed, wondering who on earth he'd bought such a hideous necklace for. His wife? She couldn't imagine a snooty society maven ever wearing something so garish. A girlfriend on the side? Much more likely, she thought, wrinkling her nose.

She looked at the name of the jeweler on the white satin under the lid. "I guess I'll have to take it to the jeweler's tomorrow." She sighed. Tomorrow was Christmas Eve—she had two houses to clean and her aunt's and uncle's party afterward. She really didn't have time to make another trip up to Michigan Avenue.

It would serve him right if I didn't return it until *after* Christmas, she thought, feeling just a little bit grinchy herself.

"This guy must be really rich." Martina glanced sideways at Ellie. "I wonder who he is."

"I have no idea." And she didn't *want* to know.

"Mmm." Martina was still eyeing her. "Some old guy, I suppose."

"Not really. Thirty, maybe."

"Thirty! That's not bad at all. Good-looking?"

"I didn't think so," Ellie lied. In fact, her first impression had been that he was very attractive. When she'd first looked up into his concerned face, her heart had given an odd little thump. He'd seemed so friendly, his greenish eyes smiling down at her…until suddenly, for no reason at all, they'd turned a frosty gray.

She'd fumed over his rudeness all the way home. She'd apologized automatically—but really, the collision had been his fault as much as hers. He hadn't been looking where he was going and he'd been walking very fast. He'd knocked her off her feet, caused her to drop and damage some of her gifts and made her miss her train, as well. He could have at least offered her a ride. Not that she would have accepted, but still… He'd probably been worried that she'd get his fancy limo dirty.

No, he hadn't been attractive at all, she realized now. "He was big with mean eyes," she told her cousin.

"Fat?"

Actually, he'd felt like solid steel when she bumped into him. "I couldn't tell—he had on an overcoat. But he had a Van Gogh sort of face."

"What's that supposed to mean?" Martina asked. "He only had one ear?"

Ellie laughed and shook her head, but didn't say any more. It was too hard to explain. In her mind's eye, she could see the man clearly, the heavy eyebrows, the penetrating eyes, the angular features just slightly asymmetrical....

"Hmmph. I don't know why rich men all have to be ugly as dirt." With a sigh, Martina reached into the bag again and pulled out the magazine she'd asked Ellie to buy. "Well, maybe not *all* rich men," she amended, holding up the magazine to show Ellie the cover. "Garek Wisnewski is a doll, don't you think?"

Ellie had grabbed the magazine at the store with barely a glance at the cover. Looking at it now, she stiffened.

Dominating the page was a picture of a half-dressed redhead and a man staring angrily at the camera—a man with familiar cold gray eyes below slashing black brows.

The expression on his face had been exactly the same a few hours ago when he'd left her standing in the gutter.

Ellie looked at the headline above the picture.

Main Course: Hanky Panky, it screamed in eye-popping red print. *Dessert: Chicago's Most Eligible Bachelor.*

Chapter Two

Getting in to see Garek Wisnewski was like trying to get in to see the pope.

Ellie had been worried that the office building might be closed on Christmas Eve, but it wasn't. Employees filled the marble foyer—at least the part Ellie could see from the security desk near the entrance while the guard inspected her ID. He looked at her license closely, as though he suspected it might be a forgery, before demanding to know her business. She told him, then waited, shivering every time someone opened the door and let a blast of cold air in, while the guard made a telephone call, casting suspicious glances at her the whole time.

As ten minutes stretched into twenty, Ellie began to be annoyed. She'd come straight here from cleaning the second house on her schedule and she felt grimy and sweaty. She needed to go home and wash and change for the party. She wanted to be at her uncle's, not standing in this cold foyer waiting on Garek Wisnewski. She wished she hadn't let Martina talk her into trying to contact him directly.

"Don't you see, Ellie?" Martina had said. "This is your chance. Return the necklace and ask him if he needs any art for his office. Maybe he'll buy something. And if you're lucky, maybe he'll ask you out on a date."

Ellie rolled her eyes. "I doubt he would appreciate anything at Vogel's. And if he asked me for a date—which he wouldn't!—there's no way *I* would agree to go anywhere with him. I told you how rude he was. Besides, what kind of man gets featured on the cover of tabloids with his 'exotic dancer' girlfriend?"

"Maybe that's why he was rude—because he was embarrassed about the picture."

Ellie glanced at the scowling face on the magazine cover—and at the redhead wearing a big smile and not much else. The caption identified her as Miss Lilly Lade and stated her occupation.

Embarrassed? Ellie didn't think so. There'd been too much hard self-assurance in his bearing. Even if he had been, that still didn't excuse his rudeness. Nor his execrable taste in women—and jewelry. Now the necklace made perfect sense.

But in the end, she hadn't been able to outargue Martina or her own conscience, which told her that if she really wanted to help everyone who relied on the gallery, she would swallow her pride and go see Garek Wisnewski.

It was the logical thing to do. No matter how rude he'd been, he'd be grateful when she returned his tacky necklace.

After looking up Wisnewski Industries in the phone book and discovering its ritzy address on the Loop, she took the train from her last job into town. When she first saw the skyscraper, it reminded her of a fortress—all gray stone with narrow, impenetrable windows.

The overzealous security guard reinforced the impression.

He finally hung up the phone and turned to her, a clipboard in his hand, his eyes still suspicious. "Fill in your name and address, and I'll give you a pass to go up. Leave your coat and things here."

Did he think she had a weapon hidden in a pocket? Ellie shed her wet coat and took the clipboard, filling in the gallery's address rather than her own. She clipped the plastic pass to the strap of her purse.

Upstairs, she had to run another gauntlet—of navy-suited, gimlet-eyed assistants. At the final desk sat a woman with shiny silver-gray hair cut like a helmet and piercing blue eyes who gazed disapprovingly at Ellie's jeans and yellow sweater. She made a brief phone call, then escorted Ellie into the inner office.

Wood paneling, plush carpet and heavy furniture met Ellie's gaze. Trite, but obviously expensive oil landscapes hung on the walls. Directly ahead, seated behind a carved mahogany desk in a thronelike chair, was Mr. Eligible Bachelor himself.

Dressed in a gray pinstripe suit, white shirt and black tie, he looked as conservative as his office, although not quite as elegant. His tie skewed slightly to one side as if he'd tugged at it, and his jacket looked a little tight across the shoulders. His clothes didn't really suit his blunt features and muscular build.

"So you tracked me down," he said.

Ellie stared into eyes as cold as the storm outside. "I beg your pardon?"

The cynical lines around his eyes and mouth deepened. "Do you think you're the first woman to engineer a meeting and come chasing after me?"

She stiffened. He thought she'd bumped into him on purpose in order to meet "Chicago's Most Eligible Bachelor?" Was *that* why he'd so abruptly abandoned her on the sidewalk yesterday?

What an ego!

Trying to control her temper, she walked forward and held out the jewelry case. "I came to return this."

He took the case and flipped up the lid. He stared at the necklace a moment, his expression inscrutable, then closed the box. Leaning back in his chair, he looked at her.

She expected him to thank her, express his gratitude, perhaps even apologize for his rudeness. But he did none of these things.

"I suppose you expect a reward," he said.

In that instant, Ellie realized she would prefer to scrub Mrs. Petrie's toilets every day for the rest of her life rather than sell anything from the gallery to this man. He sat there, making no effort to stand or invite her to sit, offering her money instead of thanks, his every action, his every word an insult. She knew this kind of man—one who cared nothing about people or their feelings, one who cared only about money and what it could buy. He would never spend his cold hard cash on something as frivolous as art. Contemporary art especially would be incomprehensible to him.

Ellie clenched her fists. Her first impulse was to refuse with icy politeness, then turn and walk out. But just yesterday she'd promised herself she would think like a businessman. Businessmen weren't polite—as Garek Wisnewski had just so unpleasantly demonstrated— and they weren't squeamish about money.

"Yes, I do expect a reward," she said with all the poise she could muster. She met his gaze directly, calmly, not blinking even when his eyebrows rose.

The corner of his mouth curled upward. "At least you're honest about it." He pulled a checkbook from his coat pocket. "How much?"

"Five thousand." She named the first figure that came into her head.

He stared at her for a long, silent moment.

Putting up her chin, she waited.

She didn't have to wait very long. With a shrug, he picked up a pen, wrote a check and held it out to her.

Taken off guard, she stared at the slip of paper. She might not have inherited the Hernandez haggle gene, but she'd thought *he* would know how to negotiate. What kind of businessman handed over five thousand dollars so easily?

"Well?"

Glancing up, she saw him watching her, his eyes narrowed. Quickly, she stepped forward and took the check. She glanced at it, seeing a five followed by the requisite number of zeros. She hesitated again, struggling with her conscience. She was about to give him the check back, when the phone rang.

Garek Wisnewski pressed a button and his assistant's voice came over the line.

"There's a delivery here from marketing," she said.

"Send it in." His gaze flickered toward Ellie.

Clearly, she was dismissed. His rudeness made her spine stiffen—and subverted her conscience. "Thanks for the check," she said airily. Stuffing the slip of paper in her purse, she headed for the door.

It opened before she reached it, and a skinny young man—a boy, really—entered, carrying a large, flat, cloth-covered rectangle. Setting it on a cherrywood table, he mumbled, "Mr. Johnson told me to bring this straight up," then bolted from the room, slamming the door behind him.

Ellie blinked at the boy's behavior. But probably all of Garek Wisnewski's employees were terrified of him, she decided, moving toward the door again.

A flutter caught her eye as the cloth slipped from the rectangle. She stopped, her eyes widening at the revealed portrait.

Or rather, at the revealing portrait.

Lilly Lade, in full-breasted, bare-buttocked, dimple-thighed glory, rose from a large white clamshell, her red hair contrasting vividly with the bright blue ocean behind her. Two leering "wind gods" hovered at one side, their expressions as crude as the artist's brushwork.

"Was there something else?"

Ellie jumped at the sound of his harsh voice. "No, not at all." But she couldn't resist adding, "I was just thinking this is exactly the kind of painting I would expect you to have." She smiled sweetly.

His stony gaze dropped to her mouth, then lifted. "You object to nude portraits?"

"No, I object to bad art."

"Ah. An expert."

The sarcasm in his voice annoyed her almost as much as his rude stare. "I work in a gallery."

"The poster store at the mall?"

"Vogel's in Pilsen," she snapped. "Specializing in

contemporary art. Feel free to stop by if you ever want to buy something with a little higher concept." Turning on her heel, she grabbed the doorknob and twisted it.

A large hand reached over her shoulder and rested against the door, preventing it from opening. Scowling, she glared over her shoulder. A broad expanse of male chest met her gaze. Quickly she looked up—a long way up. He was bigger than she remembered. How had he managed to cross the room so quickly and silently?

He loomed over her, staring down at her with narrowed eyes. "I've already paid—I'm not paying any more. Anything else you want to offer me will have to be for free."

Outrage stiffened her spine. "There's nothing I want to offer you," she said, yanking at the doorknob. It didn't budge. "Will you please take your hand off the door?"

His gaze wandered over her, lingering on her mouth. "If you change your mind, contact me—but first use that money to buy some clothes that have a little 'higher concept.'"

He released the door, and she yanked it open, angry enough to spit paint, and stormed out.

When she arrived home at her apartment, she went inside and slammed the door.

Martina came out of the bedroom, dressed in velvet pants and a red sweater, her head tilted as she put a dangling earring in her ear.

"You're back!" she said. "I was beginning to worry. How'd it go?"

"Fine." Ellie thrust her coat and boots into the closet, then stalked into the kitchen. "Although I'm thinking of writing a letter to the *Chicago Trumpeter*."

Martina, following her into the kitchen, blinked. "You are?"

"Yes, to tell them they made a mistake about Garek Wisnewski." Ellie took the five-thousand-dollar check from her purse, shoved it in the junk drawer and slammed it shut. "They should have named him Chicago's Most *Obnoxious* Bachelor."

It might have been Christmas Eve with most of the country in festive spirits, but Garek wasn't sharing their happy mood. As far as he was concerned, the day was the culmination of a perfectly rotten month.

The painting of Lilly Lade—Ted Johnson in marketing's infantile idea of a joke—had been annoying. The Hernandez woman witnessing the delivery, on top of taking him for five thousand dollars, had been galling. But neither of those compared with the torture that he now endured—Christmas Eve with his sister, Doreen.

"I went to a gala at the country club," she commented as a maid poured wine in Garek's glass. "All the right people were there. The Mitchells, the Branwells. Even the Palermos. Their nephew Anthony asked Karen to dance."

"Anthony Palermo is a total geek," Karen said, the first words she'd spoken during the meal. "He has hands like wet gym socks and breath like week-old dog food."

"Karen!" her mother exclaimed. "You mustn't talk about Anthony like that. The Palermos are one of the most wealthy and distinguished families in Chicago. You should remember that."

Karen lapsed back into a sullen silence that lasted until the unappetizing meal was finished and Doreen led the way to the living room, where a mountain of presents was piled under a twenty-foot gold-and-silver tree. Karen fell to her knees and started ripping open packages. Garek retrieved a slim, flat case from under the tree and handed it to his sister.

Doreen seated herself in a red-brocaded wing chair and unwrapped the gift with admirable restraint, unsealing each taped seam carefully, without any visible excitement. But when she saw the contents of the jeweler's case, a spark lit up her usually cold gray eyes. "Ahh," she said.

On the other side of the room, the sound of ripping paper stopped. Karen came and peeked over her mother's shoulder.

"Good Lord!" she exclaimed, staring at the emerald-and-ruby necklace. "You must have spent a fortune, Uncle Garek!"

Doreen's mouth pursed. "Karen, don't be crass."

Her shoulders hunching, the girl returned to the tree. She opened another present—a notebook computer from Garek. Her face completely expressionless, she set it aside.

Doreen, whose gaze had followed her daughter, barked, "Karen…what do you say to your uncle?"

"Thank you, Uncle Garek." Karen's monotone had as much enthusiasm as a zombie's. Surrounded by the presents she'd opened—piles of clothes, tennis gear, skis, jewelry, purses, shoes—she looked under the now-empty tree. "Is that all?" she whined.

Doreen glared at her daughter. "Karen, I don't like your tone. Or the expression on your face. If you can't look and sound more pleasant, then go to your room."

"Fine." Tucking the computer under her arm, Karen headed for the door.

"I don't know what's the matter with that girl," Doreen said in a loud voice before her daughter had even left the room. "I've told her over and over again that she must be polite to you. Although I can't blame her for being disappointed. Whatever possessed you to buy a computer?"

Frowning, Garek watched his niece leave the room. "At Thanksgiving I heard her say she wanted one."

"I wish you would have spoken to me first. We already have a computer. Girls her age prefer feminine things—like jewelry."

Garek thought of the conversation he'd overheard on his last visit. Karen had been talking on the phone, telling some unseen person that she *desperately* wanted a new computer. "I think you underestimate Karen."

Doreen stiffened. "I believe I'm better acquainted with my own daughter's likes and dislikes than you. You barely know her."

That was true. He'd been close to Karen when she was younger—she'd been bright and funny and interested in everything. But since becoming a teenager, she'd changed. She'd grown about ten inches into a tall, lanky brunette with a pale complexion and hostile brown eyes. Only rarely did he catch a glimpse of the curious, affectionate child she'd been.

"I'm afraid those terrible friends of hers are having a bad influence on her," Doreen continued. "One girl's father is a truck driver! If only I could send her to a decent school, instead of that horrible one she's attending now."

"You can afford it." Garek walked over to the tree, looking at the jumble of gifts Karen had left behind. "If you want to."

Doreen almost dropped the necklace. She snapped the box closed and glared at him. "You don't know what it's like to have your beloved husband die and be reduced to living in poverty—"

"Come off it, Doreen." Garek nudged the tennis racket with his toe, then bent down and picked it up. He took a practice swing. Lightweight, perfectly balanced, the racket sliced through the air. "Grant divorced you long before he died. And he paid through the nose to get rid of you. If he'd been smart, he would've made you sign a prenuptial agreement."

"I would never sign something like that—I would be grossly insulted if he'd even asked. Besides, I deserved every penny I got in the settlement. It wasn't my fault he fell for that little slut. I should have gotten more. But I never get my fair share. Just look at Wisnewski Industries. It's not right that Father left the company to you and…and for heaven's sake, must you swing that racket? Those ornaments are all Lennox crystal and they cost a fortune. If you break one, I'm going to be very upset—"

"The company was bankrupt."

His comment successfully diverted her from the safety of her ornaments. "A temporary setback, nothing more. The company is making millions now."

"Of which you, as a major stockholder, receive a very large portion. I know, since I sign the checks."

She sniffed. "I can barely maintain my position with those paltry dividends. I'll never get my name into the Social Register at this rate."

"What the hell is the Social Register?"

"It's a book listing the names of an elite group of people. The right kind of people. Like the Palermos. Ones that have a certain background—"

Garek couldn't believe his ears. "Our grandparents

were peasant Polish immigrants. Is that the kind of background you're talking about?"

Doreen's nostrils quivered. "Ancestry is only one of the considerations. There are other ways to qualify— like founding a charity for some worthy cause. Ethel started a foundation for the symphony."

"You hate the symphony."

Doreen gripped the arms of her chair. "Just because you have no appreciation for music, don't assume no one else does—"

"Okay, okay." He shrugged. "If you want to give money to the symphony, fine. Just don't ask me to make a donation."

A flush mottled her cheeks. "I shouldn't have to ask you. It's the least you could do. That disgusting picture of you and that…that dancer person has undoubtedly hurt my standing with the Social Register committee—"

"I said no, Doreen."

"Very well." Lines radiated from her pinched lips. "I'm not going to argue with you. If you won't help me set up a foundation, I'll just stick to my regular activities with the Women's League. Did I tell you Nina Lachland is on a fund-raising committee with me? She tells me a lot about her husband's business. She told me Wisnewski Industries is trying to buy out the Lachland Company, which was news to me."

He kept his stance relaxed, but inwardly he tensed. "So?"

"So, did you know there's another company interested in buying Lachland? Her husband doesn't like this Ogremark very much—"

"Agramark."

"Ogremark, Agramark, whatever. But he might

change his mind if he found out that you're having trouble finding financing for the purchase."

Garek stopped swinging the racket. "Are you trying to blackmail me, Doreen?" he asked very softly.

She smiled. "Of course not. I don't know why you would say that."

Garek didn't smile back. Acquiring Lachland was key to his plan for expanding Wisnewski Industries. Unfortunately, Agramark Inc., a subsidiary of the Calvin G. Hibbert conglomerate, was also pursuing the small shipping company. The conglomerate had all the advantages: financial resources far beyond his own, connections to key players, high-powered lawyers to deal with the legalities. In spite of all this, Garek was determined to make the acquisition and was close to succeeding.

If Doreen didn't sour the deal.

How the hell had she found out about his difficulty with the financing? He gave her a long, hard look. "I warn you, Doreen, don't interfere with my business."

"Business, business, business. That's all you think about. It's time you did something for your family. Is that so much to ask for? I don't want much—all you need to do is sponsor a foundation for me."

"Is that all?" he asked ironically.

"Actually, now that you mention it, no. I also want an assistant from Wisnewski Industries to handle all the details—I can't because of my delicate health."

Doreen was as healthy as a draft horse. She had a similar bone structure to his, with big hands and feet. When she was younger, she'd had a plump, curvaceous figure, appealing in an earthy sort of way. After she married Grant Tarrington, however, she'd lost every spare ounce of fat in an effort to look more "delicate." Unfortunately, the weight loss only made her look harsh and angular.

"I also want you to stop sabotaging my efforts to be included in the Social Register," she continued, warming to her subject. "Stop dating disreputable women and find a nice, respectable girl. Someone like Amber Bellair. I talked to her yesterday and we agreed…"

"You agreed what?" Garek asked very quietly.

"You needn't sound so nasty. We just agreed that you seem…lonely."

His grip tightened on the tennis racket as he thought of all the plans he'd made and the hours he'd put in to make the Lachland acquisition happen. Once he signed this deal, he could…well, not relax, exactly. But maybe the pressure would ease up some.

He didn't want to risk losing this deal. But he sure as hell wasn't going to let Doreen think she could get away with this kind of manipulation every time she wanted something.

"The only problem is that Ethel may not like me setting up a competing foundation," Doreen said, drumming her manicured nails on the arm of her chair. "She can be a little spiteful. She might even block my Social Register nomination. Perhaps I should find something else to support. Something cultural. Like the ballet. Or art. Art would be very classy. We could open a gallery on Michigan Avenue. Or better yet, River North—"

"A gallery?"

"To exhibit the work of the artists we sponsor. Some up-and-coming young people recommended by the Institute. Not any of those trashy modern artists, but young men and women with real talent…"

She went on, but Garek was no longer listening. He was remembering the woman who'd returned the necklace—Eleanor Hernandez. What was it she'd said? *I work at a gallery…specializing in contemporary art… feel free to stop by if you ever want to buy something with a little higher concept.*

A greedy little witch—as greedy as Doreen—only with a pair of bright blue eyes and the sexiest mouth he'd ever seen….

"I don't think I'm being unreasonable, Garek. You can afford it. It wouldn't hurt you to show a little generosity, you know. I am your only sister—"

"Very well."

Doreen gaped, her jaw sagging in a way that counteracted the most recent efforts of her plastic surgeon. "You'll do it?"

"Do I have a choice?"

"No. For once, you're going to have to do what I want."

Any of the businessmen who'd dealt with Garek Wisnewski would have been highly suspicious—if not downright skeptical—of his sudden acquiescence. But Doreen only smiled smugly, visions of how her name would look printed in the Social Register dancing in her head.

She didn't even notice the way her brother adjusted his grip on the tennis racket and executed a neat and deadly backhand.

Chapter Three

"It's your best work ever."

Tom Scarlatti's brown eyes lit up behind the thick, round lenses of his glasses. "You think so, Ellie? My roommate said it looked like a two-year-old painted it."

Ellie studied the canvas propped against the gallery counter. Although he'd used her as a model, the final result bore no discernable resemblance to her. But the free-flowing curves and vivid colors created a sense of space and harmony that was arresting.

"Your roommate is an engineer," she pointed out. "He knows nothing about art."

"That's true." Tom's narrow chest expanded a bit. "Actually, I do think *Woman in Blue* turned out well. I really hate to sell it."

"If you want, I can put a Not for Sale sticker on it," she offered. "Although I'm sure you could get an excellent price for it."

Tom reached out and touched the edge of the canvas with the very tips of his fingers, gently, tenderly. But then his hand dropped limply to his side. "I've got to sell it," he said with a sigh. "My landlord is threatening to evict me. He's a very unpleasant man. He doesn't understand about art at all—"

The bell jangled as someone entered Vogel's. Tom stopped talking, looking toward the door. Ellie turned, a smile forming, only to freeze when she recognized the man walking toward her.

Garek Wisnewski.

What on earth was *he* doing here? It had been a week since the ugly scene in his office, and she'd done her best to put him out of her mind. But she couldn't help thinking about him every once in a while—like when she'd gone to her cousin Vincente's house last weekend and saw his daughter wearing the tiny tennis shoes she'd bought her for Christmas. Or when she'd seen the towering gray walls of Wisnewski Industries through the train window on her way to a job a few days ago. Or when she'd looked in the junk drawer this morning and seen the crumpled five-thousand-dollar check shoved in the back that she hadn't quite been able to bring herself to cash, ruthless businesswoman or not.

Every time she thought of him, she remembered the ugly necklace and his rudeness when she'd returned it, and she grew angry all over again.

She clutched the gallery keys lying on the counter, wishing she'd locked the door. Had he come here to make another crude proposition?

"Excuse me," she muttered to Tom, moving out from behind the counter.

Tom sidled toward the door. "I'd b-better go," he murmured.

Ellie restrained an urge to grab his arm and cling to him—she didn't want to be left alone with Garek Wisnewski. But she couldn't do that to Tom. Tom was painfully shy around most people, and well-dressed, high-powered businessmen were the type he most dreaded.

Did Garek Wisnewski always wear a suit? she wondered as she approached him. His clothes made a valiant effort to give him a civilized veneer. They couldn't disguise, however, the grainy texture of imminent five-o'clock shadow on his jaw—evidence of barely restrained, more primitive male tendencies.

Like predation. Intimidation. Domination.

"Good evening, Mr. Wisnewski." She kept her tone polite, but cool. Not an easy feat considering the way her senses were humming on full defensive alert. She was conscious of her own clothes—a red cashmere sweater with a tendency to pill, a short black skirt, black tights and chunky black platforms. "May I help you?"

He eyed her consideringly—probably planning to give her some more wardrobe advice, she thought angrily.

"I'm just looking." He turned his gaze to a flat glass case filled with dirt and trash. "So this is 'high-concept' art. Very impressive."

She bristled at his sardonic tone. Few of the general public recognized or appreciated the skill and creativity that went into contemporary art. A lot of people snickered or looked scornful when they first came in. Usually, though, after she explained a little about the piece and the artist's concept, most viewed the work with more respect.

She didn't bother to explain anything to Garek Wisnewski, however. Why waste her time? He'd obviously come to mock her. Didn't he have better things to do?

Apparently not. He moved on and she followed closely behind, glaring at his big hands clasped behind his broad back—he was so bulky, she didn't trust him not to knock something over. Although he did walk gracefully, she admitted grudgingly to herself, his shoes making almost no sound on the polished wooden floor.

He gazed at an antique water pump resting on a square glass case filled with lightbulbs. Another lightbulb sprouted from the spigot. His eyebrows rose halfway to his dark combed-back hair.

His expression infuriated her. "It's time for me to close." She struggled to keep her tone polite. "Perhaps you could come back some other day."

"I'll only be a few more minutes," he told her, then proceeded to stroll around the gallery as if he had all the time in the world. He eyed the various pieces, his mouth curling in the same sardonic smile she'd noticed in his office. He even laughed at Bertrice's recycled-trash sculpture of a giant cockroach, although he tried to cover the sound by coughing.

He stopped in front of the counter, looking at the painting Tom had just left.

"I'll take this one."

She blinked, wondering if she'd misunderstood. "You want to buy *Woman in Blue*?"

"Yes." He arched an eyebrow at her. "Is there a problem?"

"No, no. I'm just surprised." Stunned might be a more accurate description. "*Why* do you want to buy it?"

"Do you question all your customers on why they're purchasing an item?"

"Not usually. But most of my customers like contemporary art."

"You think I don't? You shouldn't be so quick to judge me." He pulled his wallet from inside his coat pocket and produced a platinum credit card. "Can you have the painting delivered to my office?"

She didn't take the card. "*Woman in Blue* won't fit with the decor of your office. Are you sure you wouldn't like something else—something that would suit your personality better?" Her gaze rested a moment on the giant cockroach.

His gaze followed hers, and his eyes gleamed, whether with laughter or anger, she couldn't tell. Anger, she hoped. But he didn't withdraw the credit card. "I prefer this one."

She didn't believe he'd come here just to buy a painting, but even if he had, she wished he would have chosen something else. She didn't want him to have *Woman in Blue*. He would never appreciate it, she was sure. She opened her mouth to refuse to sell the painting to him, then paused.

Hadn't she just recently vowed to think like a businesswoman? To sell to anyone who came through the door? Could she in good conscience refuse the sale when the gallery—and Tom—needed it so much?

The answer was unpalatable but obvious.

With the very tips of her fingers, she took the credit card and rang up the sale. "Thank you, Mr. Wisnewski," she forced herself to say. "It will be delivered first thing tomorrow."

"Excellent." He glanced at his watch, then at her.

"Ms. Hernandez, I need to discuss something with you, but I know you're anxious to close. Will you have dinner with me so we can talk?"

She stiffened. So he *had* come here to proposition her again! "No."

"It's important," he said, not even blinking at her refusal. "It concerns the gallery."

"What about the gallery?" she asked.

"Come to dinner with me, and I'll tell you."

"Why can't you tell me here?"

"I never discuss business on an empty stomach."

His smile made her even more suspicious. It was the kind of smile that made a woman want to smile back, that made her want to do whatever its owner asked—and oh, didn't he know it!

"If you're not interested," he said when she didn't respond, "I can always find another gallery." He took a step toward the door.

"Wait!"

He paused and she bit her lip. She knew he was manipulating her—but her curiosity was too great to resist. "Let me get my hat and coat and lock up," she muttered.

He didn't have the limousine tonight. Instead, he had a big black Mercedes with soft leather interior. She paid little attention to the luxury, however.

"What about the gallery?" she asked again when they were driving down the street. "Do you want to buy another painting?"

"Not exactly." He turned a corner, avoiding a snowdrift that had spilled out into the street. "Do you own the gallery?"

"No, Mr. Vogel does."

"Ah, then perhaps I should be talking to him."

"Not really. He hasn't been active in managing the gallery since his wife died. He's elderly, and his health is frail, so he lets me run the gallery for him. He trusts me completely."

"Does he? Then obviously I needn't have any qualms."

The dry note in his voice made her bristle, but before she could respond he spoke again. "I'm sorry, but I need to concentrate on my driving. I'll explain everything over dinner."

The request was a reasonable one. The road was treacherous, covered with ice and full of potholes, and the pounding sleet made the visibility poor. But in spite of the conditions, Ellie didn't quite believe him.

At the restaurant, they were quickly seated at a table with white linen tablecloths, china and crystal.

"Have you been here before?" he asked.

"No. Look, what's this all about?"

He picked up the wine list, his eyebrows rising. "Are you always so impatient?"

"Only when someone is being extremely evasive."

His eyes gleamed again in that odd manner. For a moment, she thought he was going to put her off once more, but then he said bluntly, "I'm starting an art foundation and I'm looking for artists to sponsor and a gallery to exhibit their work. I think Vogel's might be perfect."

Ellie leaned back against the cushioned seat and stared at him. Her heart started to pound. A foundation—it could make a world of difference to the gallery. She could hire art photographers, place ads in expensive magazines, attract the notice of critics and collectors who could transform an unknown artist like Tom into an overnight sensation. She could replace the lighting, fix the elevator and install a sculpture garden on the roof the way she'd dreamed....

The waiter came to the table. While he explained the prix fixe menu for the day, Ellie tried to rein in her excitement. There were a thousand galleries in Chicago, and after speaking with them, what were the chances Wisnewski would choose Vogel's? Not very high. She needed to convince him that Vogel's would be the best choice for his foundation to sponsor.

After the waiter left, she leaned forward again. "Vogel's would be ideal," she said earnestly. "Our goal is to encourage a climate of excitement, inquiry and dialogue for progressive art. We look for unconventional pieces that are conceptual and theoretically based. You won't see similar works at other galleries. Everything we handle is unique. The artists are all extraordinarily creative and innovative. Tom Scarlatti, for example, the man at the showroom when you came in earlier. He painted the canvas you bought. I'm sorry I didn't introduce you. He's a little shy. But I can arrange for you to meet him another time—"

The sommelier approached the table. Ellie tried to contain her impatience while he discussed with Garek the appropriate vintage to complement their meal. Finally the wine had been decided, the bottle brought and the ritual of pouring and tasting finished, and she was able to continue. "With the right kind of support, I believe Tom could become an important new force in the art world—"

"You appear to think very highly of this Tom Scarlatti," Garek interrupted.

"Yes, I do." She picked up her wineglass. "He's brilliant, a genius in his own way—"

"Is he your boyfriend?"

The wine halfway to her mouth, Ellie paused. She stared at the man sitting across from her.

Cool gray eyes stared back.

"No," she said slowly. "Why do you ask?"

"Just curious. Surely you must have a man in your life?"

"Not that it's any of your business, but no, I don't." She set the wine down and gave him a direct look. "I'm not interested in having a relationship right now."

The corners of his mouth twitched at her thinly veiled rebuff. "You want to concentrate on your career? I'm surprised."

"Why?"

"Because most women, no matter how much they deny it, are still more interested in finding husbands than in building their careers."

She didn't like his cynical tone or the implied criticism of women. "Really? I've experienced exactly the opposite. Most of the men I meet are desperate to get married. Especially the older ones—the ones your age."

He straightened a little. "I'm twenty-nine," he said curtly.

"Oh?" Lowering her eyes to conceal her smile, she picked up the wine again and sipped it.

There was a small silence as she drank. "Only a year or two older than you, surely," he said.

She set down her glass abruptly.

The waiter returned and placed a dish on the table. "Baby leeks cooked in their own juices," he announced.

"Just what we needed," Garek said blandly.

Ellie couldn't help laughing. "I'm twenty-four," she admitted. Then, vexed with herself for revealing even this small piece of personal information, she returned to business. "About the gallery—"

He shook his head. "You don't need to tell me any more about it. I've already made up my mind. And I've decided on Vogel's."

For a second, she thought she must have misheard him. But at the same time, she knew she hadn't. Joy burst inside her. Vogel's was saved! She wanted to dance on the table, sing at the top of her lungs, reach across the table and kiss Garek Wisnewski right on the mouth….

Almost as if he could read her mind, his gaze dropped to her lips.

Her mental celebrations came to a screeching halt. He'd looked at her mouth that way in his office. Right before he told her to contact him if she wanted to "offer" him something.

She leaned back in her seat, her smile fading.

What was going on here? This was Garek Wisnewski, the obnoxious jerk who'd knocked her over in the street and grossly insulted her when she came to his office. Garek Wisnewski, the arrogant, money-grubbing businessman who did nothing without calculating the profit. What was the catch?

Judging from the way he was looking at her mouth, she suspected she knew exactly what the catch was.

The waiter returned with more food. Ellie waited until he left before she asked quietly, "And what do you want in return?"

Garek took a bite of the Iowa lamb loin and chewed for what seemed like an awfully long time. "That's an odd question," he finally said. "Why does anyone start an art foundation?"

"Because they love art."

"And you don't think I do?" He offered her some of the braised legumes, but she shook her head. "I told you not to judge me too quickly," he said.

He was being evasive. Why? "Why *my* gallery? You don't even like me."

His eyebrows rose. "What gave you that idea?"

"You weren't exactly polite when I returned the necklace."

"I apologize for that. Women who seek me out tend to have an ulterior motive."

"They want to get their picture in the paper?" Ellie guessed.

"They want to get married."

Ellie choked on her goat cheese and bleeding-heart radishes. The poor man obviously suffered from a serious medical condition—paranoia conceititus. "I have no desire to marry you, I promise."

He smiled, but with a slight cynical lift to his lip. "That's why I chose your gallery—you're honest enough to admit that it's the money you care about."

She opened her mouth, then paused. She doubted she could make him change his mind about her—and if she tried, he'd probably accuse her of trying to make him fall in love with her or something else equally ridiculous. "What exactly will this foundation do?" she asked instead.

"The usual. Exhibits—shows, I believe you call them?—featuring the gallery artists. I'll send an assistant to the gallery tomorrow. She'll report to you, and you can tell her whatever needs to be done. I also want you to work with her to arrange a special pre-opening event, a silent auction, to be held at my sister's home. I would expect you to choose the art, naturally."

Ellie took a sip of the heady wine, considering which of the artists she should feature. Tom, without a doubt, and Bertrice. And maybe Carlo Bustamente—

"I would expect you to attend the silent auction, of course," Garek continued. "And I'll need to take you to the symphony this Saturday—"

"The symphony!" She set down her wine. "I understand the silent auction. But why the symphony?"

"I'm going to have to introduce you to art collectors. There will be quite a few at the concert."

"Why can't you bring them to the gallery?"

"I run a business. I don't have time to run a shuttle service."

What he said made sense—almost. She suspected the whole art foundation was a ploy of some kind. To get her to go to bed with him? That seemed pretty far-fetched. He was rich—and not completely unattractive. Surely he could find some woman to overlook his warped personality without going to so much trouble. More likely he needed a tax write-off. Or maybe he was a frustrated artist and needed a place to exhibit his paint-by-number masterpieces….

Her hand jerked as a terrifying thought occurred to her, causing her almost to knock over her wine.

"That portrait I saw in your office…" She tried to sound casual, although everything inside her was recoiling with horror. "The one of Lilly Lade—did you paint that?"

He looked startled. "Good God, no. Why do you ask?"

"No reason," she lied, leaning back to allow the waiter to take her plate. She rested against the cushioned chair, her terror receding—although not completely. She knew Martina would tell her to plaster the gallery walls with hundreds of portraits of Lilly Lade if that's what it took to get him to agree to use Vogel's for his foundation, but Ellie couldn't do it. She couldn't allow someone like Garek Wisnewski to distort the gallery into something unrecognizable.

"If I agreed to this," she told him, "I would have a few conditions."

"What conditions?"

"First, I must have complete control over the direction and focus of Vogel's. I have the final say in all decisions. Nothing is exhibited unless I agree."

"That's fine. I don't want to change anything about the gallery. It's perfect the way it is."

She searched his expression but couldn't detect any sarcasm in either his voice or face. "Second, this is business, nothing else."

"Naturally. What else would it be?"

She frowned, but all she said was, "You accept the conditions, then?"

"That's all? You don't want me to get your name in the Social Register?"

She stared at him. "I beg your pardon?"

"Never mind. Yes, I accept your conditions."

"Then I accept your offer," she said solemnly.

"Thank you."

She couldn't help smiling at his slightly ironic tone. He smiled back, and she felt the same pleasant jolt she'd felt the first time she'd met him.

She squashed the feeling immediately. This was Garek Wisnewski, she reminded herself. Sure, he could be charming when he wanted, but that didn't change the fact that he personified arrogance and conceit. And in spite of his agreement to her conditions, she didn't really trust him. She couldn't shake the sense that he had some hidden agenda, some secret purpose that he wasn't telling her. He was up to something.

But what?

Chapter Four

Garek detested the symphony. When he felt compelled to attend for one reason or another, he usually escorted Doreen or Amber, but they enjoyed it as little as he did. Amber pretended to like the music but always seemed more interested in looking around the theater from their balcony seats to see who was there than in anything happening onstage. Doreen, whom he suspected of being tone deaf, usually fell asleep about halfway through, her head lolling in time to the flutes. During the intermission, neither Doreen nor Amber ever mentioned the concert. Instead, they estimated the cost of Buffy Vanderhorn's designer gown and speculated as to whether Tritia Mitchell's jewelry was real or fake.

Therefore, it was something of a shock to discover that Eleanor not only listened to the music—she listened with intense concentration.

He stared at her, frowning slightly. Seated next to him

in the darkened theater, she seemed very small, the top of her head barely reaching his chin. She appeared as fragile and breakable as the strings of the violins being played onstage—and yet, her back was as straight as the conductor's baton.

The evening wasn't turning out the way he'd expected. When he'd picked her up earlier, he'd been stunned by her appearance. From the top of her carefully arranged curls, to the beaded silver sheath that hugged her curves, she looked utterly gorgeous.

He'd told her so, but to his annoyance, his voice was husky, like a teenager's on his first date.

"Thank you," she'd responded coolly. Distantly. *Regally.*

She'd kept up her air of nonchalance until they were actually in their seats and the music started. Then her indifference disappeared.

The light from the stage illuminating her expression, he watched as her eyes glistened with each blare of the French horns and her lips trembled with each screech of the violins. The notes and chords, meaningless to him, obviously enthralled her in some way that he couldn't begin to fathom.

By the time the curtain went down for intermission, her face was glowing—until she caught him looking at her. Then her expression cooled again. "I've always liked that particular conductor," she said as he escorted her out to the lobby. "He can elicit music from an orchestra like no one else."

"You sound like an expert."

"Do I?" She shrugged, the movement drawing his attention to her creamy shoulders covered only by a gauze wrap. "Actually, it's been a long time since I've been to a symphony. I listen on the radio sometimes. Do you come very often?"

"Occasionally." The light from the chandelier caused her silver dress to gleam, making it difficult not to stare at her—as he noticed several other men blatantly doing. He put his hand on her elbow and directed her toward the bar. "Some of the people I do business with sponsor the symphony. I have to make an appearance once in a while. Would you like some champagne?"

She gazed at him searchingly. "Do you ever do anything just for fun?"

She sounded half disapproving, half curious. "There's no time for fun if you want to succeed in business," he told her. "You're competing to stay alive in a ruthless environment. But the reward is huge."

She accepted a glass of champagne from him but didn't drink. "Money, you mean?"

He nodded.

Her mouth formed a little moue of distaste, drawing his gaze to her pursed lips, but before she could say anything, a booming voice called his name. Turning, he saw Ethel Palermo bulldozing her way through the crowd, her meek little husband, George, trailing behind. With an inward sigh, he introduced Eleanor, but Ethel paid little attention.

"Is your sister here?" she demanded.

"I haven't seen her."

"Hmmph." Ethel's snort was full of disapproval. "I talked to her this afternoon. She said she was leaving on a cruise tomorrow and had to finish packing. I reminded her how important it is to support the symphony, and she said she would try to come."

"Maybe Doreen succumbed to one of her headaches," Garek said. "She has them frequently, you know." Most frequently when faced with the thought of spending three hours at the symphony.

"Hmmph." Ethel adjusted the diamond tiara nestled in her silver, beehive hairdo, then inspected Eleanor with sharp eyes. "Eleanor Hernandez? I've never heard of you."

With an easy smile, Eleanor responded, "There's no reason you should have."

To Garek's surprise, she continued, conversing pleasantly with the older woman. After just a few minutes, Ethel was telling "Ellie" about her three sons—all of them ungrateful slobs—her daughter—a constant source of disappointment—and her ten grandchildren—all amazingly beautiful, intelligent and talented. When Ethel revealed that the oldest showed a remarkable talent for art, Ellie mentioned her gallery experience and talked about ways to encourage the child.

"Although talent is often inherited, it must be nurtured," she said seriously. "Are you or your husband creative?"

Ethel nodded. "I've always liked art. And George plays the violin."

Ellie turned to George, a smile lighting her face. "You do? My father also played. What did you think of the soloist?"

"I thought his improvisation was weak. It lacked passion."

"Oh, no! The passion was there. It was just very restrained—very subtle."

"Subtle?" A spark lit up George's normally glazed blue eyes and his nasal twang grew more pronounced. "Nonexistent, I thought…"

Perhaps it was just a fluke, Garek thought as he listened to George happily dissecting the performances of the whole orchestra, that Ellie had managed to charm the most difficult couple in Chicago.

But the same thing happened with the Branwells, the biggest snobs west of the Mississippi, and again with the Mitchells, a couple whose doomsday conversation would scare even the most determined optimist.

"You seem to be enjoying yourself," he said in a neutral tone of voice when they were alone for a moment.

"Yes, I am."

"You certainly handled the Palermos well. I've seen veteran society hostesses tottering off in a daze after an encounter with them."

"Oh?" She rearranged her shawl over her arms. "I found them very interesting."

"Interesting?" He couldn't keep the disbelief from his tone. "George and Ethel Palermo?"

She tilted her chin a little. "Yes—why not? George is virtually an expert on the symphony, and Ethel had a lot of interesting insights on her family."

"And the Branwells and the Mitchells? Did you find them *interesting*, as well?"

She nodded, then looked at someone behind him. He turned to see Jack Phillips, an old business acquaintance, approaching—along with a tall, thin blonde dressed in black satin.

"Garek, darling!" Amber Bellair cooed. "Where have you been? I haven't seen you in ages!"

Garek shrugged and performed the introductions.

Amber looked Ellie up and down dismissively, then turned back to Garek. "Why don't you ever call me anymore? I've been terribly lonely."

"You told me you never wanted to see my face again."

"*Darling*...I was *joking*. You can always call me." She drew a French-manicured fingernail down his chest. "Anytime."

"Sorry, Amber, that won't be possible." From the corner of his eye, Garek watched Eleanor smile at something Jack said to her. "I'm very busy."

"Busy with Ms. Hernandez, I suppose."

He turned his gaze back to Amber's narrow, aristocratic features. "I'm sponsoring an art foundation through the gallery where she works," he said evenly. "Our relationship is purely professional."

Her mouth curled in a sneer for the blink of an eye, then disappeared, leaving her face smooth and blank. "I understand."

What she understood was questionable, but the bell sounded, cutting off their conversation. The crowd started moving toward the theater doors.

"It was a pleasure meeting you, Jack." Ellie's warm smile faded only slightly when she turned to Amber. "And you, too, Ms. Bellair."

Amber waved her hand carelessly, barely glancing away from Garek. "Darling, when you get tired of... working so hard, give me a call."

She strolled off, and Garek escorted Eleanor toward the theater doors.

"Ms. Bellair is a good friend of yours?" Ellie's voice was almost as cool as Amber's had been.

"Not exactly." He tried to increase their pace, but the crowd made it impossible. "We dated for a while."

"But you broke up?"

"She was getting a little too...serious."

"I understand," she said, in much the same tone as Amber had a few minutes ago. He looked at her sharply.

Her expression was bland. "You don't want to give up being Chicago's Most Eligible Bachelor."

He flinched as she said the stupid title out loud. "Hardly," he snapped.

She made a slight choking noise. She didn't smile, but her eyes gave her away, and he scowled. "It's not funny," he told her.

"No, of course not," she agreed, coughing.

"That idiotic newspaper article has caused me more grief than you can possibly imagine." He stepped back to allow her to precede him into the row.

She didn't move, the laughter in her gaze gone. In its place glimmered a different emotion, a softness…sympathy?

She touched his arm lightly. "Money must be an awful burden in your relationships."

The muscles in his forearm contracted at the brush of her fingertips, even as he blinked at her words. He'd always found money to be a great advantage. "Why would you say that?"

"Because…oh, I'm so sorry, ma'am!" Ellie stepped forward into the row of seats to allow a woman with sharp elbows to pass.

Garek followed Ellie, turning sideways, to shuffle past the patrons already seated. He waited until they reached their own seats before asking again, "Why would you say that?"

"What? Oh," she whispered as the lights dimmed and the curtain rose, "just that it must be terrible to have women interested in you only because of your money."

The music started, and she turned her attention to the stage.

Ignoring the opening strains, Garek stared down at her.

Amber obviously hadn't believed him when he said his relationship with Ellie was purely professional, but it was true. He would never be interested in someone as venal as Eleanor Hernandez—she was merely a means to an end.

Still, he couldn't help feeling a niggling annoyance, as he sat through the second half of the concert, that she would assume that women were interested in him *only* because of his money.

Chapter Five

Garek took Ellie to a French restaurant the following week. The tuxedoed waiter seated them in the atrium, a secluded area lit by candles, decorated with flowers and featuring a magnificent view of the city skyline. The decor was elegant, the clientele exclusive and the prices exorbitant.

Naturally, Ellie thought wryly as she ate wild Atlantic salmon and Alsace-style cabbage and listened to Garek explain a few details of the art foundation. He was obviously used to the best. Which boded well for the foundation. He would make it a success, she was positive. She should be deliriously happy. And she would be, if it weren't for one thing. Him.

She looked at the hard angles of his face, listened to the authority in his voice as he recited facts and figures. He had the kind of self-confidence that came from knowing he could make his own way in the world without help from anybody. She might have admired the trait, envied it, even—if she hadn't met his ex-girlfriend. It was hard to envy a man who'd been involved with a woman whose eyes were as cold and calculating as Amber Bellair's.

"Any questions?" he asked as the waiter set plates of chocolate-raspberry torte in front of them.

A million, she thought, glancing away from his strong features. Were all the women he knew like Amber Bellair? Did they all look at him like an investor assessing a potentially profitable enterprise? Were they all like painted photographs, flat and artificial?

"No," she said, fiddling with her fork.

"I received the assistant's report. She said you've been extremely busy this last week."

Ellie nodded. Preparing for the silent auction and the show took a lot of time. She'd been able to quit her housecleaning jobs since Garek was paying her a generous salary—almost too generous. She couldn't quite shake the suspicion that he had some ulterior motive. But although she'd tried several times to question him, he remained evasive. He wasn't one to reveal a lot about himself.

"Would you like to go over the budget figures?" he asked.

"No, thank you."

His eyebrows rose.

"I've always preferred art and music to math," she felt compelled to say. "Balance sheets give me a headache."

"Didn't you say Martina was studying business?" he asked. "Perhaps she could go over the numbers for you."

He'd met her cousin when he'd picked Ellie up earlier that evening, and they'd seemed to hit it off immediately. Martina had tossed her mane of long dark hair and smiled flirtatiously at Garek while Ellie got her coat. "You better snap him up quick, El," Martina had whispered in her ear before they left, "or someone else will. If only I didn't have a boyfriend!"

Ellie picked up her fork. "That's really not necessary," she murmured to Garek before taking a bite of the torte.

"You think she won't be able to understand it?"

Ellie bristled immediately. "I'm sure she would. She's graduating in June, a year early. She's absolutely brilliant."

"Is that so?" His mouth curved upward at her defense of Martina, but he didn't pursue the subject of the budget. "Martina said you're from Philadelphia," he said instead.

"Did she?" What else had her cousin said? Ellie wondered uneasily.

"Do your parents still live there?"

"They died in a car accident when I was thirteen."

She said it matter-of-factly, but the long-ago loss still had the power to cause a dull ache in her heart.

"I'm sorry," he said quietly. "That must have been difficult for you."

She turned away from his steady gaze and looked out the window at the city lights sparkling in the cold, dark night. She didn't want him to be sympathetic. "Fortunately, I had relatives who took me in." She looked back at Garek and forced herself to smile. "What about your family?"

"My father died of a heart attack eight years ago. My mother remarried and moved to Florida a few years later. I rarely see her. There's just my sister and me. And my fifteen-year-old niece."

Her breath caught. Even less did she want to feel sympathy for *him*. But it was impossible not to. He recited the facts as unemotionally as she had, but she knew only too well how pain could be hidden under a facade.

"Are you close to your niece and sister?" she asked, resisting a foolish urge to reach across the table and touch his hand.

He shrugged. "I don't have a lot of time. Work keeps me busy."

His response should have banished all sympathy for him, but it didn't. After her parents died, she'd lived with her grandfather, but she'd called her aunt and uncle and cousins almost every day and stayed with them every summer. They'd filled a terrible void in her life. Apparently Garek's business had performed that function for him.

But that was his choice, she reminded herself. He could have chosen to reach out to his sister and niece. "You should make time," she said quietly.

He sipped his coffee. "Thinking of starting an advice column?"

She ignored his gentle mockery. "I think it's a mistake to put work before family."

"But what if your family depends on you to work to make money?"

She frowned. "Your sister and niece depend on you financially?"

"Not exactly. I'm speaking more hypothetically."

"Every situation is different. Everyone must make their own choice." She twirled a bite of torte in raspberry sauce. "I just think sometimes people end up regretting their choices."

"Hmm," he murmured noncommittally. "Tell me more about your family."

She doubted he was really interested, and she didn't want to get drawn into talking about her grandfather and the messy details of their estrangement, but she went ahead and told him about her uncle Rodrigo and aunt Alma and their six children. The three older were all married with children of their own.

"Then comes Martina, then Roberto, then Alyssa," she continued. "Alyssa is about the same age as your niece—she'll be fourteen in March."

"How long have you shared an apartment with Martina?"

"About a year. Ever since I moved to Chicago. I was broke and there aren't a lot of high-paying jobs for art history majors—"

"You have a college degree?"

"Yes, a master's. Why do you look so surprised?"

"No reason. Is your cousin Roberto still in high school?"

"No, he graduated last year." Just in time to get himself thrown in jail. But she wasn't going to tell Garek that. "He's very sweet. Sometimes he takes his machismo a little too seriously, but he has the kindest heart of anyone I know. He'll play cards with Grandma Pilar for hours, even though she cheats and can't always remember his name. He can be a little impulsive sometimes, but he always means well. He's very protective of me."

"Do you need protecting?"

"No, of course not. Although Robbie thinks so. Probably because of…" She paused, vexed with herself for talking too much.

"Because of Rafe?"

She straightened. "How do you know about him?"

"Martina said I was a 'vast improvement over Rafe.' Your ex-boyfriend, I take it?"

"Mmm." She was definitely going to have to have a talk with Martina. "I brought him to Chicago to meet everyone. Martina and Robbie didn't like him. And it turned out they were right."

"Rafe broke your heart?"

"No, he just toughened it up a bit." She felt his gaze on her face. Afraid he would ask her more questions, she added lightly, "Everyone has to have at least one failed love affair. Even you, I'll bet."

He had to think for a while. Either he'd had so many, he couldn't remember, or he'd never been in love. She wondered which it was.

"There was Monica Alexander," he finally said. "I was madly in love with her."

"What happened?"

"She dumped me when my father died and his business declared bankruptcy. I had to leave college to sort out the mess."

She grew still, watching him from wide eyes. "How terrible."

Garek looked amused. "It wasn't a huge tragedy. In fact, it was probably the best thing that could have happened to me. I was able to focus all my attention on the business."

"But you must have been terribly hurt—and at a time when you needed her the most."

He shrugged. "I survived."

Obviously. But at what cost? Was that when he'd acquired the air of cynicism that marked his features so strongly now? Was that when he'd begun to have so little faith in people—especially women?

The meal finished, he drove her home and walked behind her up the outside stairs to her apartment. "The Institute of Art is having a private opening of their new exhibit tomorrow night," he said. "I've arranged for tickets. I'll pick you up at seven."

More networking, Ellie thought, stopping in front of her door. And more time spent with Garek Wisnewski. "Wasn't the symphony enough?"

"I thought you would like going to the art show."

She would *love* to go, despite a slight lingering doubt about his motives. Once again, how could she refuse? "Okay. Thanks." She smiled at him.

His gaze narrowed a bit and drifted over her.

"What?" she asked, her smile faltering.

"You've got salt on your coat. Hold still."

Glancing down, she saw him brushing at a gray mess on her side. She must have grazed against the spray of salt and ice on his car, she realized.

She swayed a little, and he put his hand on her shoulder, holding her firmly as his gloved fingers swept along her hip, removing the last traces of dirty salt, his touch brisk, efficient, impersonal. When he finished, he released her, said good-night and left.

She watched him until he got in his car and drove off.

An uneasy feeling curling in her stomach, she went inside.

Chapter Six

Stacy Hatfield, the assistant Garek had assigned to work on the foundation, was bright, enthusiastic and very young—barely eighteen. Ellie would have enjoyed working with her if it weren't for one thing—the girl had a huge crush on Garek Wisnewski.

Ellie's own feelings were growing more and more confused. During the last week and a half, he'd taken her to the art show, several dinners, a play and a basketball game. She kept reminding herself that their relationship was purely business, but sometimes, for a moment or two, she would forget. She'd lain awake all night thinking about him, her thoughts going round and round in circles, until she swore she wasn't going to think about him at all. But that was difficult to do when Stacy talked about him constantly.

At the gallery, Ellie tried to escape the girl's chatter by going upstairs to the framing studio, but Stacy merely packed up her laptop and followed.

"Mr. Wisnewski's the best employer I've ever had," Stacy said, her fingers flying over the keyboard. "Actually, he's the only employer I've ever had, unless you count Mrs. Bussey, whose kids I baby-sat when I was fourteen—she had a nervous breakdown after she had her fourth child in six years—but everyone at the company agrees that Mr. Wisnewski is the best. He is so generous. I told him he was paying you way too little, and he said to double your salary."

Startled, Ellie looked up from the long, thin piece of oak she was pretending to inspect. "Stacy! I can't accept that!"

"Of course you can. You deserve it. You've been working like a dog."

It was true—she *had* been working long hours. But accepting a raise didn't feel right. If Mr. Vogel had given it to her, she wouldn't have objected. But Garek...

"Did you have a good time at the game?" Stacy asked. She had an amazing ability to talk and type at the same time at a combined speed of approximately eight hundred wpm.

Ellie sat down at the miter box with the piece of oak molding. "It was very nice. We had courtside seats, we ate catered food in a private box at half time, and the Bulls won." She'd enjoyed herself at the game. Afterward, though—

"Are you going out with him on Saturday?" Stacy asked, her fingers flying across the keyboard. "It's his birthday, you know. He's going to be thirty. Kind of old, but he's so gorgeous, I almost don't care."

Ellie hadn't known. Why hadn't he told her?

"How is the catalog for the silent auction coming along?" she asked, hoping to divert the girl.

"Fantastic. The pictures the new photographer took of the art turned out great. He also took a picture of Mr. Wisnewski and Mrs. Tarrington, Mr. Wisnewski's sister, to send to the newspapers to help publicize the event. I was surprised Mr. Wisnewski agreed to that. He hates any kind of publicity."

Ellie usually subdued any impulse to question Stacy about Garek, and she tried to restrain her curiosity now. But somehow, she couldn't stop herself from saying, "Oh?"

Stacy needed no further encouragement. "Ever since being named Most Eligible Bachelor he's been hounded by women," the girl said. "I read in the *Chicago Trumpeter* that a woman waited for him in a parking garage, then jumped on the hood of his car and started kissing the windshield. She left red-lipstick imprints all over the glass before he could get her off. Another woman broke into his house and stole all his underwear and put it up for sale on eBay. The police caught her and arrested her, but not before she'd sold a pair of boxer shorts to a woman living in a Florida retirement community. He threatened to sue the *Chicago Trumpeter* and they've backed off for the last month or so, but we still get women calling or coming to the office on some pretext, hoping to meet him."

Ellie bent over the miter box, the whine of the saw ringing in her ears as she remembered Garek's surliness when she'd bumped into him on the sidewalk. What had he said in his office the next day? *So you managed to track me down.*

She still couldn't really excuse his rudeness to her. But she could understand it. She even sympathized with him in a way—she hated the press, also.

She didn't want to like him. She didn't want to be *aware* of him. But it was hard not to be. At the art show, she'd been conscious of his hand at the small of her back as he guided her from painting to painting, his bulk protecting her from being jostled by the crowd. When he took her to dinner, she was conscious of his hands on her shoulders as he helped her off and on with her coat. At the play, a comedy, she'd been distracted several times by his deep, rather rusty-sounding laugh; that had been bad enough, but then afterward, she'd neglected to button her coat before they went outside. Greeted by a blast of icy cold wind, she'd started to tug off her gloves, but he'd grabbed her hands and pulled her into a sheltered doorway. "I'll do your coat up for you," he'd said, and proceeded to fasten each button from her throat to her hemline.

She'd tried not to let his closeness affect her. She'd tried to ignore the increasingly familiar curling sensation low in the pit of her stomach. Just as she'd tried, a few days later, at the basketball game, not to notice the way his hair grew to a point at the nape of his neck; the way he listened silently, intently, to what she said; the masculine scents of wool and leather that clung to him; and the amusing contrast of the floral scent of his hair.

A gift of shampoo from his niece, he'd said when she impulsively asked about it last night after inviting him into her apartment for coffee. Sitting next to her on the couch, he'd immediately put down his cup and leaned over to sniff her hair.

"Mmm, strawberry, I think." He lifted a strand of her hair and ran it through his fingers.

Her entire scalp prickled at his touch. He continued to stroke her hair, his fingers gradually weaving their way deeper and deeper into its thickness until he was cradling her head, holding her completely still as he stared down at her mouth with a dark, intense look in his eyes.

Her heart pounded against the wall of her chest as if trying to get out. She knew she should pull away. She knew letting him kiss her was opening the door to all kinds of trouble. But the feeling inside her didn't respond to arguments. The feeling wasn't logical. It wasn't sensible. It was just there. Hot and needy and demanding. One kiss, it told her rational self. Just one kiss....

"Ellie? Ellie? Is something wrong with the frame?"

She came out of her trance to find Stacy staring at her. "The frame?" Ellie repeated stupidly before she remembered. She looked at the angle she'd cut into the oak. "Oh, yes. I mean no. It's fine. I'm sorry, I wandered off for a moment there."

A knowing smile appeared on Stacy's face. "I understand. I'd be in a daze too if Garek Wisnewski was in love with me."

"Stacy, please!" Ellie felt her cheeks heating up. The girl was too romantic...and too naive. "Garek Wisnewski isn't in love with me. He and I are just friends."

She bent over the miter box again, with another piece of molding. Friends...she tested the word in her head. How else to describe their relationship? It wasn't just business, anymore, she couldn't deny that. But they weren't really dating, either. If they had been, surely he would have kissed her last night when she'd made no move to stop him.

But instead, he'd released her and headed for the door. She'd felt bereft, confused. Had she misread the look in his eyes when he looked at her mouth? She'd never liked her mouth. In school, the other kids had teased that her lips were "upside down." Maybe he stared only because of their odd shape....

He'd paused by the door and looked down at her, frowning. "I'll pick you up at seven on Saturday." Then, as suddenly as he'd abandoned her, he'd pulled her to him and had pressed a hard, swift kiss against her mouth, before striding out the door.

That kiss…it had been so brief, over almost before she realized what he was doing. Even so, she couldn't stop thinking about it. Rafe's most passionate embraces had never affected her the way Garek's fleeting kiss had.

"I didn't even know about his birthday," she said out loud to Stacy. "I don't really know him that well. And he doesn't know me."

"He knows enough," Stacy said. "And what else do you need to know about him except that he's a hunk?"

What he was thinking. Feeling. What he thought about *her.* "This is a ridiculous conversation," she told Stacy.

"I heard him tell his sister on the phone that he wanted to introduce you to her soon—"

Ellie's heart skipped a beat. "You shouldn't repeat things you overhear," she reprimanded the girl, but not with as much conviction as she should have.

Stacy ignored her. "Garek's sister is very important to him. I heard that the necklace he bought her for Christmas cost a fortune. Emeralds and rubies are very expensive."

The girl nodded in a knowledgeable manner, but Ellie barely noticed. He'd bought that necklace for his *sister?* He hadn't talked about Doreen Tarrington much, but he must care for her to buy her such an expensive piece of jewelry. Granted, he had terrible taste, but still, it had been kind of him.

Garek Wisnewski, *kind*?

"Technically, his sister is in charge of this art foundation," Stacy continued. "But her health isn't too good, so he won't let her do any work. She loves art. He started the foundation for her."

The piece of wood in Ellie's hands splintered. "He did?"

"Yes, Mr. Wisnewski's secretary, Mrs. Grist, told me all about it," Stacy said. "His sister told him she wanted to start an art foundation and Mr. Wisnewski agreed to finance it for her."

Ellie remembered her suspicion when Garek had proposed investing in the gallery. Why hadn't he admitted it was for his sister?

She remembered something he'd said. *You shouldn't be so quick to judge me.*

Ellie picked up a fresh piece of wood. "That was very…kind of him," she said slowly.

Garek was hard at work late Friday afternoon when the phone rang. Impatiently, he glanced up, his eyes burning from reading the small, tight print of a contract. He had a stack of documents he needed to go through and sign in order to finalize the terms for financing the prospective buyout of Lachland, and he wanted to finish today.

"Yes?" he said curtly into the phone.

"Mrs. Tarrington's here to see you," his assistant told him.

Ah, Doreen. He looked down at the contract he'd just signed. The deal with Lachland hadn't closed yet, but the financing was in place. Doreen didn't know it yet, but her ace had been trumped.

Garek smiled. "Send her in, Mrs. Grist."

Doreen came in, wearing a black designer dress with a black-and-white scarf pinned at her shoulder that had the unfortunate effect of making her look sallower than usual. She carried a flat, rectangular box in her black-gloved hands.

"Happy birthday, Garek," she said, kissing the air by his cheek, then settling herself into the leather chair opposite him.

He sat back down and opened the box. "A tie," he said. Mustard yellow, emblazoned with a coat of arms, it was uglier than the muddy green one embroidered with a well-known designer's initials that she'd given him last year. It was even uglier than the putrid maroon-and-gold one she'd given him the year before that, the one she'd accidentally left the half-price sticker on.

"I traced our family tree back to Polish royalty," Doreen said. "This is our ancestral crest."

Garek almost laughed. The Wisnewskis were descended from pure peasant stock and Doreen knew it. But he allowed no trace of his thoughts to appear in his expression. "Thank you, Doreen. How was your cruise?"

She coughed a little and her normal foghorn voice weakened. "The cruise was horrible. We sailed through a hurricane and I was sick the whole time. Karen was heartless—she reminds me of you. She had no sympathy for my illness. She lounged around the pool the whole time, flirting with the crewmen. I complained to the captain about allowing employees to fraternize with the guests…but never mind about that." Her gaze sharpened on him. "I spoke to Ethel this morning. She said she saw you at the symphony with some woman. And at the art exhibit. And at the Cape Cod Room."

"Ethel ought to be a reporter for the *Chicago Trumpeter*." Garek half rose from his chair. "If that's all, Doreen—"

"No, that's not all, Garek Wisnewski! Who is this woman?"

Garek reseated himself, biting back a smile. "Her name is Eleanor Hernandez."

"Hernandez—that sounds Mexican."

"So it does."

Silence fell in the office.

Garek leaned back, waiting for the explosion. Doreen had complained frequently about the influx of Mexican immigrants, ignoring him when he pointed out their own grandparents' parallel circumstances.

Finally, Doreen broke the silence. "I'm glad to see you're keeping up your end of our bargain."

He frowned. "I beg your pardon?"

"Our bargain," she repeated. "To start dating a nice girl. Ethel told me she is a perfectly charming young woman."

Garek made no response. At that particular moment, he was incapable of one.

"Ethel also said that she received an invitation to the silent auction for the art foundation. She told me—confidentially, of course—that her friend on the Social Register committee is very impressed by the foundation. He made a note when Ethel mentioned it to him. It's possible I'll be listed in the summer edition. Ethel said it's going to press in a few weeks—"

"Doreen," Garek cut her off. "I have to get back to work." Ignoring her indignant sniffs, he escorted her out of his office, then returned to his desk and sat down, frowning. His plan to teach Doreen a lesson had gone crazily awry. But then, a lot of things hadn't gone the way he'd expected in the last few weeks. Ever since he'd met Eleanor Hernandez.

His gaze drifted to the canvas hanging on the wall opposite his desk.

Woman in Blue.

He'd intended to give the painting to Ted Johnson—payback for the Lilly Lade painting—but instead, on some incomprehensible impulse, he'd ordered it hung on his office wall.

The painting had an oddly compelling quality. He stared at it, trying to comprehend its appeal, but without success. The random daubs of color, the splotches and squiggles didn't make any sense—just like Ellie.

He couldn't quite figure out what she wanted. He'd thought at first it was money, pure and simple, but she wasn't very consistent about it. When he'd taken her to the art show and she'd admired a small ceramic vase, he'd offered to buy it for her, but she'd refused. Even more surprising, when he'd given her a raise, she'd tried to refuse that also. He'd disregarded her protests, but still, he found her actions odd. She must be after something else. But what? Publicity for the gallery? Definitely. But there had to be more than that. Something just for her. Fame?

Maybe. Although it was hard to believe that someone who could smile the way she did could be so calculating. When Ellie smiled, her eyes smiled also, and her whole face glowed. Warmth practically radiated from her. Sometimes when she smiled, he found himself liking her…like a friend. Although friendship wasn't what he'd felt a few nights ago when he'd stood at her apartment door, looking down at that siren mouth of hers. He'd wanted to rip off her clothes, throw her down on the floor and make hard, sweaty love to her until neither one of them could move….

Hell.

He frowned at the painting on the wall, then bent back over the contracts on his desk. Going out with Ellie was business, an extreme measure undertaken to protect Wisnewski Industries. Once he'd closed the Lachland deal and his sister found out he'd tricked her, he wouldn't need to spend any more time with Ellie. No more froufrou art shows or la-di-da symphonies. He planned to make a quick, clean break with Eleanor Hernandez, and he had no intention of complicating the matter by getting involved with her.

No intention at all, he told himself again later that evening as he rang her doorbell.

Martina, dressed in boots, a denim skirt and an emerald blouse that flattered her dark hair and eyes, let him in.

"Big date tonight?" he asked her.

She flashed a bright smile. "My boyfriend is coming to get me and we're driving up to Madison."

"Madison? That's a long trip in this weather."

"Yeah, we're going to spend a couple of nights with some friends of his. Go ahead and sit down. Ellie's not quite ready yet."

He sat on the sofa, talking casually with Martina while some part of his brain filed away the information that there would be no one in the apartment when he brought Ellie home tonight; it would be completely empty. Quiet. Private.

Not that it mattered.

He forced himself to focus on Martina. She had a flirtatious, sensual manner—except when she talked about business. Then she was as coolheaded as any of his vice presidents. He'd had a chance to talk to her several times in the last couple of weeks, and he liked her.

"What do you think of Ellie's new acquisition?" Martina asked, waving a hand at the artwork resting on the coffee table.

It looked like a lump of mud. "Very unusual."

Martina snorted. "It's a piece of crap, that's what it is."

Eyeing the brown mass, Garek wondered if she meant the remark literally.

"But half the stuff she brings home is crap," Martina continued. "Just let some crackpot wander into the gallery and tell her some sob story and she immediately opens up her purse. Just because her father was an artist and could never sell any of his work, she feels compelled to buy something from everyone."

Garek frowned, but before Martina could say anything more about Ellie's father, he heard footsteps behind him. Standing, he turned to see her coming from the bedroom. For a moment, all he could think of was how gorgeous she looked. A scrap of blue velvet clung to her breasts, waist, hips and thighs, emphasizing her smooth curves.

"Happy birthday!" She smiled up at him and held out a box that he hadn't even noticed she was holding.

A flat, rectangular box.

Her smile made accepting the box a bit less painful. He opened it and stared down at the tie within.

Green musical notes floated down the length of it. The widest part featured miniature newsprint with a headline: PUKE ON NUKES. The whole thing appeared to have been splattered with a rainbow of paint.

"How…colorful," he said.

"It's a bit outrageous," she admitted, glancing at his face a trifle anxiously. "But I thought you ought to loosen up and try something a little less conservative than the ties you usually wear."

"Did an artist from your gallery design it?" he asked.

"Not exactly. I haven't displayed any of his work. But he came into the gallery last week and he's trying very hard to get established…"

He looked at her, then at Martina, who rolled her eyes before discreetly disappearing into her bedroom.

Suddenly, Garek wanted to laugh. Struggling to keep a straight face, he looked back at Ellie. "Then you'll have to help me put it on, won't you?"

Her radiant smile made the sacrifice worthwhile.

He pulled off his old tie, and bent his head so she could put the new one around his neck. His movement brought his face into close proximity with her bare shoulders and he inhaled the scent of the light perfume she wore. All desire to laugh disappeared. Straightening back up, he put his hands on her waist to steady her—or perhaps himself, he wasn't sure.

Her waist felt tiny within the grasp of his hands. The tips of her breasts were only inches away from his chest. The slightest tug would pull her up against him….

"There you go." She stepped back abruptly.

His hands fell to his sides and he looked down at the knot she'd tied with amazing speed and skill. "You've done this before."

"I always tied my grandfather's for him." She sounded a little tense. "Let me get my coat and we can go."

The club he took her to was small and dark and intimate. On the dance floor, she moved with a sensual Latin grace that sent his temperature soaring. He couldn't take his eyes off her. The clinging blue dress made him want to run his hands from her shoulders down to her hips. He managed to restrain himself for at least an hour—until the band finally decreased the tempo and played a slow dance. He pulled her into his arms.

She hesitated; then, her arms lifted around his neck and she moved closer, her breasts pressing against his chest.

Missing a step, he steered her into another couple. He recovered quickly, however, and tightened his arms around her. His hands slid down over her hips. She made no objection, just squirmed closer.

He groaned. He was in heaven. And hell. He wanted to get the hell out of there, take her back to her apartment and—

"Garek," she murmured.

"Hmm?"

"I know why you started the art foundation."

He stiffened slightly. "You do?"

"Yes. I know you're doing it for your sister." She leaned back to smile at him. "Why didn't you tell me? I think it was a very kind and generous thing to do."

Garek stared into her shining eyes. "I'm a businessman," he said. "I'm never kind or generous."

Still smiling, she shook her head and rested her cheek against his shoulder. He looked down at her soft hair, a whirl of thoughts in his head. She didn't believe him, obviously. What would she say, he wondered, if he told her that he had started the foundation only to annoy his sister, not to please her? What would she say if he told her he didn't care at all about pleasing his sister; but that the idea of pleasing *her* was becoming more and more appealing?

Involuntarily, he tightened his arms around her. He'd

drunk too much wine. That was why he was having these puerile thoughts....

A sudden, bright flash nearly blinded him. Blinking as his vision slowly cleared, Garek saw a man with a camera hurrying toward the door.

Annoyance raced through him, but then he sighed. Actually, he was surprised it hadn't happened sooner.

"Hope you don't mind having your picture in the paper," he said lightly, glancing down at her.

Shock and dismay fluttered across her face. "Aren't you going to try to stop him?"

"I can if you want me to."

She nodded mutely.

He caught the man just as he was climbing into a car. After a brief scuffle, Garek managed to get the camera. As he stripped out the film, the photographer said, "Aw, give a guy a break. My editor said she'd give me a bonus if I got this picture."

"Get the hell out of here," Garek snapped. "Before I decide to take you apart, as well."

The reporter gave Garek an appraising glance, then got in his car, apparently deciding retreat was in order. "Can't blame a guy for trying," he yelled out the window before driving off.

Garek made his way back into the restaurant.

"Did you catch him?" Ellie asked anxiously when he was close enough to hear.

"All taken care of." He looked at her pale face and put his arm around her. "C'mon. Let me take you home."

Driving down the dark, icy streets, they didn't talk much. Garek thought about the incident in the club and Ellie's reaction. She should have been delighted about that picture. She could have parlayed it into publicity for the gallery and thus for herself. What kind of sane person turned down such a golden opportunity?

He stopped the car in front of her apartment building and looked at her.

"You didn't introduce me to any clients tonight," she said.

"No," he said.

There was a slight pause.

"Would you like to come in for some coffee?" she asked.

The streetlight haloed her face, emphasizing her wide, clear eyes and sweetly smiling lips. Maybe she was as honest and genuine as she appeared. The only problem was—he didn't want her to be. He didn't want to be attracted to her. He didn't need to complicate this situation any more. If he had any sense at all, he would let her go up to her apartment alone….

He looked at her, all soft-eyed and dewy-lipped.

That mouth.

"I'd love to come in," he said.

Chapter Seven

As they stepped into the apartment, Ellie pulled off her glove and reached out to turn on the light. Before she could do so, however, Garek's hand closed over hers. He'd taken off his gloves, too, and his fingers were warm. He shut the door, cutting off the glow from the porch light and casting the apartment into complete darkness. Ellie stood perfectly still, the blackness pressing against her, the scent of damp wool, icy wind and male musk filling her nostrils. Outside the apartment, the savage sleet and wind howled; inside, all was quiet—except for the wild beating of her heart.

His arms came around her, he pushed her against the door, and he kissed her.

The darkness whirled around her. His mouth was hard against hers, the intensity of its demand shocking.

She put her hands on his chest to push him away, but then the kiss changed. It became gentle, tender.

She hesitated. She'd wanted him to kiss her. *Really* kiss her. She'd been curious ever since that frustrating half kiss he'd given her the night of the basketball game. And now she knew. She knew…oh, dear heaven! She knew it felt wonderful to be kissed by Garek Wisnewski. He was so big, she would have thought he would crush her, but he held her so lightly, so gently, it was like being cradled in a cocoon. But at the same time, there was nothing soft about him. His body felt hard and muscled, his lips firm against hers. Rippling sensations flowed over, around and all the way through her. She liked being kissed by him. She liked the way his mouth felt on her lips and her chin and her neck….

She felt his fingers undoing the buttons of her coat; his hands burrowed underneath, stroking her sides. That felt good, too. She reached up, entwining her fingers in his hair, pressing herself closer to him.

His hands slipped down the velvet of her dress to her waist, then up to the undercurve of her breasts, then down to the tops of her hips. And then back up again until his thumbs were resting against the sides of her breasts.

She was aware, suddenly, that she was on the verge of breaking some tenuous thread of restraint, of allowing herself to go beyond what she'd intended. She'd only wanted to know what it was like to kiss him. She hadn't intended it to go any further than that. She hadn't expected to feel like this. To want him so intensely…

But she did. She didn't care about anything else. She only wanted the kiss to go on and on…she wanted him to touch her breasts. She wanted him to touch her all over—to make love to her….

The door suddenly pushed against her back, thrusting her forward. Garek held on to her, stepping backward, pulling her with him. The light flashed on, blinding her as a familiar voice said, "Something's blocking the door...oh!"

Ellie blinked at Martina, who stood openmouthed in the doorway, her boyfriend behind her.

"Martina! What are you doing here?" Aware, suddenly, of Garek's arms around her, Ellie stepped away from him.

Martina's wide-eyed gaze flickered back and forth between Ellie and Garek. "The road was snowed under...we're going to drive up tomorrow afternoon instead...I'm really sorry, I didn't mean to interrupt!"

"You're not interrupting." Ellie wondered if she looked as self-conscious as she felt. "Hi, Billy. Come sit down."

"Uh, thanks, but I have to go," he muttered with an uneasy glance at Garek's stony face. "See ya tomorrow, Martina."

"Bye, Billy." Once Billy left, Martina started sidling toward her room. "Uh, I'm really tired." She faked a yawn. "I better go to bed now. Good night!" She scuttled the last few steps into her bedroom.

Garek turned back to Ellie, his eyes dark and intense. "Come to my apartment with me." His voice was low and husky.

"No." She glanced away from his compelling gaze.

He cupped her face in his hands, forcing her to look at him. "Have dinner with me tomorrow night, then. At my apartment."

The expression in his eyes made her tremble. She knew she should say no. She had to say no. She opened her mouth to say no.

"Yes," she whispered.

A light blazed in his eyes and he gave her a quick hard kiss. "Until tomorrow."

And then he was gone.

Chapter Eight

Ellie found it difficult to concentrate on work the next day. She hung a painting, moved a sculpture and worked on balancing the accounts. Unfortunately, she hung the painting upside down, dropped the sculpture—the head broke off—and could not get the accounts to balance no matter how many times she checked the numbers.

Finally, she gave up all pretense of working and sank onto the flat, leather bench that sat in the middle of the gallery so people could sit and look at the art. Coincidentally, it also gave her an excellent view of the clock. Three fifty-eight. Three fifty-nine. Four o'clock….

In one hour she could go home and get ready to go to dinner at Garek's.

And to make love.

The words had been unspoken, but she'd heard them loud and clear all the same.

Was she insane?

She must be.

How else could Garek Wisnewski have affected her like this? Last night, she'd felt hot inside and out, she'd yearned for his touch, she'd forgotten all caution, all logic, all common sense….

How had he done that to her?

After he'd left last night, she'd sat in a daze on the couch in the living room, not moving until she heard the creak of a door hinge. Glancing over, she'd seen her cousin cautiously stick her head out. "Is he gone?" Martina had whispered.

Ellie had nodded.

Martina had opened the door all the way and come out into the living room. Clad in a long flannel nightgown with pink bunnies on it and a fuzzy bathrobe, she'd sat cross-legged on the couch next to Ellie.

"Wow," she'd said. "You look like you've died and gone to heaven. He must be one heckuva kisser."

"Martina…"

"Oh, come on, El…fess up. I can't believe what I just saw. You haven't so much as looked at a man since you came to Chicago. I was beginning to think I was going to have to send your name to the nearest convent."

Ellie had frowned. "Just because I don't jump into bed with every guy I meet doesn't mean I want to be a nun."

"Yeah, yeah." Martina hadn't been put off by Ellie's discouraging tone. "Garek Wisnewski, of all people! I thought you hated him."

Ellie had thought so too. But something had changed in the last few weeks. "He's not as bad as I thought," she'd admitted. "He makes me laugh. He can be really kind. He cares a lot about his sister—"

"Ellie…" Martina had stared at her, a frown knitting her forehead. "Are you in love with him?"

The question had rasped on Ellie's skin like an ice scraper. "No, of course not," she'd said automatically.

"Yeah, right," Martina had said. "I believe that one."

"It's true," Ellie had insisted. "I'm not in love with him."

"Well, you should be. You should forget about that loser, Rafe—he never cared about you. He was only out for what he could get. Garek is different. I've seen the way he looks at you. I think he's in love with you. Or if he's not, he will be soon." Martina had yawned. "I've got to get up early. Good night."

Ellie had gone to bed soon after Martina, but she hadn't slept well.

Are you in love with him?

Fourteen hours later and the question was *still* echoing inside her head.

Ellie closed her eyes, blocking out her view of the ridiculously slow-moving clock. Was she in love with Garek? She didn't think so. And yet, she'd never felt like this before, not even with Rafe. With Rafe, she'd felt an odd mix of excitement, curiosity and rebellion. With Garek, she felt excitement, too, but it was fueled more by a genuine liking of him as a person. Rafe had talked a lot, but rarely backed up his speeches with action. Garek, on the other hand, spoke very little, but he accomplished everything he set out to do. Rafe had ridiculed her interest in art and music. Garek wasn't necessarily a devotee of either, but he obviously recognized the importance of both and shared her deep commitment to supporting artists and the arts. Rafe hadn't cared about his disabled father and ailing mother—she hadn't even known of their existence until he broke up with her. Garek obviously cared deeply about his family—he supported his sister and gave her loving, thoughtful gifts. Like the necklace. And the art foundation…

If she let the relationship continue on its natural course, if she went to his apartment and had sex with him, she would probably fall in love with him. But would he love her in return?

Martina seemed to think so. But Ellie wasn't so sure. She thought about how badly Rafe had hurt her. She didn't want to go through that again.

And yet, in more ways than one, she'd been hiding ever since she came to Chicago. She couldn't live the rest of her life this way. At some point she was going to have to take a risk on someone.

Maybe it was time to take that risk….

She looked at the clock.

Four fifty-seven. Four fifty-eight. Only two more minutes….

The door opened and a woman entered. She wore a royal-blue designer suit, her hair fresh-from-the-salon styled and tinted, a large diamond on her finger. She had that too-perfect look of plastic surgery and could have been anywhere from thirty to fifty years old.

Usually Ellie would have been delighted at the arrival of a customer, no matter how close to closing time. But today she only wanted to hurry home and get ready to go to Garek's.

With an effort, she hid her impatience. "May I help you?"

"I am Doreen Tarrington," the woman announced.

Doreen Tarrington…Garek's sister?

Ellie smiled, warmth curling inside her. Had he sent his sister to meet her? "Mrs. Tarrington! How nice to finally meet you. I'm Ellie Hernandez, and *this* is Vogel's Gallery."

Doreen did not smile back. Nor did she take Ellie's outstretched hand. Haughty gray eyes gazed disdainfully around the room, and as she looked at several of Ellie's newest purchases, a horrified expression settled on the woman's features. "I *knew* it. I *knew* it!" she said bitterly.

Ellie's hand dropped to her side. The warmth inside her faded. "Is something wrong?"

"I would certainly say so—this place is ghastly! This isn't *real* art! What will the Palermos and the Branwells think? He did this on purpose. I know he did!"

"Who?" Ellie asked.

"Garek." Loathing filled Doreen's voice. "My brother. He picked this gallery to humiliate me. The wretch. The terrible wretch!"

Ellie's stomach knotted. "Mrs. Tarrington, you don't know what you're saying. Garek did this for you—"

Doreen laughed cynically. "Is that what he told you? You obviously don't know him very well. Or do you?" The piercing gray gaze, suddenly looking very much like Garek's, swept over her. "He's sleeping with you, isn't he? A common sales clerk! I can't believe Ethel was taken in by you—or Garek, either. But of course he wasn't. I see it all now. I make a perfectly reasonable request that he start an art foundation for me, and what does he do? He seeks out the trashiest gallery he can find just to annoy me. How like him. How very like him!"

Ellie opened her mouth to say something—anything—but Doreen continued, her anger as biting and unstoppable as the wind over Lake Michigan.

"And you—I suppose you're the 'suitable girl' I asked him to find." Doreen's hard gaze swept over her again. "How much did he pay you to play this horrible trick on me? Or did you do it for free, thinking he really cared about you? I hope you weren't that naive. The only thing my brother cares about is himself. And money, of course."

Without another word, Doreen turned on her heel and left the gallery. Ellie, feeling dazed, went into her little office and sat down. She stared at the canvas over her desk. It showed an artist drawing the barren landscape outside his window—only in his rendition everything was green and in flower.

Ellie had always liked the painting. It reminded her to look on the bright side. But now it seemed to have a totally different meaning.

Had she been looking at everything through rose-colored glasses—seeing only what she wanted to see?

She picked up a pitcher of water, but her hands were shaking so badly, she put it back down.

That woman—that horrible woman was Garek's sister? She obviously didn't think too highly of her brother. Could what she'd said be true? Had Garek chosen Vogel's and gone out with Ellie to *humiliate* his sister?

Ellie clasped her hands together tightly. She didn't want to believe it. But it all rang true. All the little inconsistencies that had puzzled her, that she'd ignored, now made terrible, sickening sense. His seeking her out for his art foundation after insulting her in his office. His quick decision to choose Vogel's without even speaking to any other galleries. His insistence on taking her to the symphony, to dinner, the art show and the basketball game....

Ellie felt cold inside. She'd thought he was a kind and generous man who loved his family. But now with that facade stripped away, she saw the same man who'd left her standing in the gutter—cold, selfish, heartless. Did he care about anyone or anything other than himself?

Money, according to his sister.

Ellie folded her arms on the desk and put her head down on them.

She should have questioned him more closely instead of allowing herself to believe the best. But that was what she'd *wanted* to believe. If Doreen hadn't come in, Ellie would probably be on her way over to his apartment right now, planning to spend the night with him....

Air burned inside her lungs, stinging her throat and nose and eyes. She'd thought she might be falling in love with him. She'd thought he might learn to love her. How could she have been so stupid?

"Ellie?"

Startled, she lifted her head. "Robbie?" Blinking back her tears, she looked at her handsome cousin standing in the doorway of her office. "What are you doing here? I thought you were still in jail."

He hunkered down next to her. "I got out early for good behavior. I only have to report to my parole officer once a week."

"That...that's great." With an effort, Ellie tried to put aside her emotional turmoil and concentrate on Robbie. He looked thinner than she remembered, and his skin had a slightly sallow cast—but his hands twitched with the same restless energy, and when she sniffled, she caught the scent of Old Spice, the cologne he'd always favored. "Have you seen Aunt Alma and Uncle Rodrigo yet?"

"Not yet. I'm not so sure they'll want to see me."

"Of course they will," she said automatically, although, secretly, she wasn't so sure about Uncle Rodrigo—he'd been extremely angry when his son got arrested. "How are you doing, Robbie?"

"Good. I've been clean for the last six months."

"That's great. I'm so proud of you."

"Thanks, El. But never mind about me. Why were you crying?" His big brown eyes, so like Martina's, were full of concern.

Ellie's shaky composure threatened to crumple under his inquiring look. She tried to smile. "Nothing, really. I was just upset about...something to do with the gallery."

"Are you crying over that Wisnewski guy?"

Ellie straightened abruptly. "Where'd you hear about him?"

"Martina said you're in love with him."

"Martina told you that!"

"Yeah. I called your apartment this morning and talked to her awhile. She told me all about you and Wisnewski."

Ellie wished they would have talked about something else. Didn't Martina know by now not to say anything about Ellie's love life to Robbie? "Well, it's not true."

He looked as though he didn't believe her.

"Really," she insisted, wiping the tears from her face. "Oh, maybe I thought I was for a minute or two, but now I know I was mistaken."

He was still staring at her, a frown on his face. "I've never seen you cry over a man before—not even that jerk Rafe."

"Robbie, this is ridiculous." She stood up. "I don't want to talk about Garek Wisnewski anymore."

Cracking his knuckles, Robbie stood also. "He hurt you."

"Yes…I mean, no, not really," she said, alarmed. She remembered what had happened the last time Robbie got that look in his eyes. He'd always been way too protective. "Don't worry. I can handle my love life. Hadn't you better go see your parents?"

The bloodlust died out of his eyes and he shuffled his feet. "Ellie, I hate to bother you when your heart is broken and all—"

"It's *not* broken!"

"—but I don't know if my father will let me in the house," Robbie said, ignoring her interruption. "I have a friend who's going out of town and he said I could stay at his place starting tomorrow. But tonight…"

"You're welcome to stay with me," she said. "Martina's going to be gone—I'm sure she won't mind if you use her room."

"Thanks, El—you're the best. Oh, and one more thing. I have a friend—another friend. He wants to be an artist. He's really talented…."

Ellie's heart sank a little. "Did you meet this friend in prison?"

"Yeah, he got busted for some pyramid scheme. But he's completely reformed—he's a real smart guy. He's taken every mail-order course there is. If you ever need an undertaker, a minister or a lawyer, he's your man."

"Uh, exactly how long has he been in prison?"

"Not that long. The thing is, he's decided he really wants to be an artist. You think you could take a look at his stuff?"

"Sure," she said listlessly. "Have him bring by some samples of his work tomorrow."

"Thanks, El. I owe you one. Say, could you give me the key to your apartment?"

She handed over the key, and he gave her a casual hug. "Thanks again, El. Oh, and listen. If you need any help, if you want me to punch your boyfriend's lights out or something, you let me know."

"I will," she told him, touched in spite of herself.

Once he was gone, she sank slowly back into her chair, imagining a confrontation between the two men—Garek getting beat up and Robbie being hauled back to jail.

She hoped she never saw Garek again. But even more, she hoped he and Robbie never met.

Ellie was sitting on her couch that evening, across from Robbie and his friend Caspar, when the phone rang. Trying to ignore it, she pretended to study Caspar's painting.

Caspar hadn't been able to wait until tomorrow to show Ellie his work, so Robbie had invited him to come over. Caspar seemed nice enough—he was a tall, thin young man with lank brown hair and a skittish gaze—but Ellie hadn't been too thrilled to find him in her apartment when she arrived home. His paintings held even less to thrill her. His bland landscapes did little to distract her from the shrill ringing of the telephone. Was it her imagination or did the phone actually sound *angry?*

"Ellie? Ellie? Are you there?" The harsh voice coming from the answering machine definitely sounded angry. "Pick up the phone, Ellie, or I'm coming over…."

Becoming angry herself, Ellie stalked over to the phone on the kitchen wall and snatched up the receiver. "I can't talk right now," she snapped. "What do you want?"

"What do you think I want?" he snarled. "I want an explanation of that message you left on my phone."

"I don't care what you want—" Seeing Robbie and

Caspar eavesdropping with blatant interest, she hunched her shoulders and turned her back to them. "I don't want to go out with you anymore, you snake," she hissed, adding a few improvements to the calm, cool message she'd left earlier. "I don't ever want to see you again, you miserable excuse for a human being. Which part don't you understand?"

"Oh, I understand you're upset about something. I just don't understand what."

"I had a little visit from your sister today. Let's just say that she opened my eyes as to your true character."

There was a long silence. Then, his voice grim, he said, "I'm coming up."

"Coming up? What do you mean?" She ran over to the window and saw him getting out of his car, cell phone in hand. "No! You can't—"

The line went dead. She saw him put the phone in his pocket and start up the stairs.

Panic assailed her. She didn't want to see him. She didn't want to talk to him. She wanted to hide. She'd get Robbie to tell him to go away....

Robbie!

Oh, dear heaven. There was no predicting how Robbie would behave.

The doorbell rang.

She wondered if there was any chance Garek would just leave if she ignored it.

The bell rang again—a long, extended ring, as if someone was holding his finger on the button.

"Robbie," Ellie said. "Could you and Caspar please go into Martina's room for a few minutes?"

Robbie frowned. "Who's at the door? That guy you're in love with?"

"I'm not in love with him!" she snapped, her patience fraying badly. "I just need to talk to him—privately."

Robbie didn't move, his frown deepening. "You're sure acting strangely, Ellie. Crying over this guy one minute and snapping at me the next—"

"She's probably pregnant, man," Caspar said. "That's how my sister was when her old man knocked her up."

"Pregnant!" A murderous rage lighting his brown eyes, Robbie took an impulsive step toward the front door.

Ellie caught his arm. "Robbie, I'm *not* pregnant!"

"My sister denied it too," Caspar said. "But five months later she had little Willard. Cute kid. Except his head was kind of pointy—"

"Oh, for heaven's sake!" Ellie couldn't take any more. "Robbie and Caspar, in the bedroom—*now!*"

Robbie looked as though he was going to refuse, but she gave him a stern look, and reluctantly he allowed her to push him toward the bedroom. "If you need any help," he said, cracking his knuckles, "just call out and I'll be glad to—"

Ellie slammed the door closed.

Taking a deep breath, she wiped her damp palms on her skirt, smoothed her hair, then marched over to the door and opened it.

Garek immediately shoved his way past her. "We need to talk."

"About what?" she said as coolly as she could. "About the art foundation you started for your sister? Doreen told me how much she appreciates your efforts on her behalf."

He gave her an unreadable look. "So?"

"So! So!" She stared at him in disbelief. "May I ask you one question? And please be honest. Did you know your sister would hate Vogel's?"

He hesitated, then answered bluntly. "Yes."

Pain lanced through Ellie's heart. She wanted to creep into the bedroom and hide. But she couldn't let herself hide from the truth any longer. She needed to know it all. "Did you deliberately choose Vogel's to annoy her?"

He met her gaze, his own level. "Yes."

The pain grew worse. "And did you go out with me for the same reason?"

"Yes."

That was it, then. Her throat was so tight, she could barely speak. "Then there's nothing more to say." Afraid she was going to start crying, she turned away.

He caught her arm, and she blinked back her tears. She couldn't cry—she *wouldn't*. Not in front of him. She yanked free of his grasp and folded her arms across her chest, glaring. "Will you please leave? You accomplished everything you set out to do."

Garek stepped back. He shoved his hands in his pockets, making no effort to defend himself. How could he? Everything she'd said was true. But somehow, at the same time it *wasn't* true. He'd certainly started out the way she said. But nothing had turned out as he'd expected. He'd wanted to spite his sister—but it had been a long time since he'd even thought of that. He disliked contemporary art—but he enjoyed listening to Ellie's enthusiasm for it. He'd gone out with her to teach Doreen a lesson—but somehow, when he was with Ellie, he forgot about his sister. He looked at her flushed cheeks and pursed lips. His gaze flickered down to her rounded breasts pushed up by her folded arms, then back up to meet her angry eyes head-on. He wanted her with an intensity he'd never experienced before. He wanted her—and he wasn't willing to give her up.

"Whatever I intended at the start of our relationship doesn't really matter anymore. Everything has changed. I didn't expect it to. I didn't want it to. But there's something between us, Ellie, something I can't deny and neither can you. Come on," he said, his voice low and seductive. "Admit it. You want me as much as I want you."

"You're crazy." Ellie glared at him, hating the arrogant certainty in his tone. "How could I want you? Everything I thought I liked about you was a lie. You don't like your family, you don't like art or music. You don't even like *me*."

"You're wrong, Ellie." His hard gaze turned dark and sensual. "I do like you."

Before she could move, he took her in his arms and kissed her. For a second, everything inside her went limp. He was right. She did want him. She did want to find out what was between them....

But she wasn't completely stupid.

With every ounce of willpower she could summon, she pulled away from him. "No, Garek. I—"

"Hey, El," a voice interrupted her. "You need some help getting rid of this jerk?"

As one, Garek and Ellie turned toward the bedroom.

Garek's eyes narrowed when he saw the stranger standing in the doorway. Pierced and tattooed, the young man had the wiry build and mean eyes of a street kid, and he smelled of too much cologne. Who the hell was he and what was he doing in Ellie's apartment?

Ellie didn't appear too pleased at the stranger's appearance either. "Robbie, I told you I can handle this myself."

"Robbie?" Garek looked sharply at her. "Your cousin, I take it?"

She didn't answer his question, all her attention focused on Robbie. "Please go back into Martina's room."

"In a minute, *prima*." The mean eyes met Garek's. "First I want to find out what this *perro's* intentions are."

"And you wonder why I prefer to keep some distance between myself and family members?" Garek drawled.

Ellie didn't look amused. "Garek, please be quiet—"

"Don't worry, El, I'll shut him up." Robbie rushed at Garek.

Garek waited until the other man was almost on him, then quickly sidestepped.

Robbie went barreling past, crashing into the coffee table and shattering the lump of mud sculpture into a thousand pieces.

"Robbie! Garek! Stop this at once!"

Robbie didn't appear to hear Ellie. A snarl on his face, he got up and hurtled back toward Garek. Garek met him with a punch to the gut, causing Robbie to double over. Garek grabbed him by the shoulders and followed with an uppercut to the jaw. Robbie collapsed to the floor.

With a shriek, Ellie rushed to her cousin's side. "Robbie! Robbie! Are you all right?"

Wincing, Robbie sat up. "I think so," he said thickly, rubbing his jaw. He glared at Garek. "Think you're pretty tough, huh? This isn't over. Not by a long shot. You're not getting away with what you did to Ellie. You're going to have to do right by her—"

"Caspar!" Ellie called out hastily, cutting her cousin off. "Come help me with Robbie!"

Garek, leaning against the door to catch his breath, watched as another man came out of Martina's room and helped Ellie support Robbie into the bedroom. Pieces of the lump-of-mud sculpture made crunching noises as the trio stepped on them, pulverizing them into dust.

"Don't worry, man," Garek heard Caspar mumble to Robbie. "We'll figure something out—"

Ellie shut the door and came back into the living room.

"Charming cousin you have," Garek said.

She glared at him. "Did you have to hit him?" she asked indignantly.

Garek folded his arms across his chest. "He attacked me."

"Well, you didn't need to be so…so violent."

Garek, recognizing a woman's illogic when he saw it, forbore to respond. Instead, he asked, "What was he talking about? What have I done to you?"

Her gaze slid away and she hunched her shoulders irritably. "Nothing. Would you please leave now? I think you've caused enough trouble for one night."

"I'm not leaving until we get this mess straightened out between us—"

The bedroom door flew open again.

Ellie turned. "What is it now—" She stopped.

Once again, Robbie stood in the doorway. Only this time, he held a gun.

Chapter Nine

"Robbie!" Ellie cried. "What are you doing? Put that gun away!"

Garek looked at the gun, then at Robbie. "Don't be a fool, Hernandez," he said coldly.

Ellie moved in front of Garek. "Robbie," she pleaded. "Remember what happened last time you shot someone."

"Rafe was an ass, Ellie. He deserved to be shot in the rear end."

Garek, tense and watchful, frowned at the name. Rafe...Ellie's ex-boyfriend?

He tried to pull her behind him, but she yanked away. "Get out of the way," he growled at her, "before your idiot cousin shoots you."

Ellie didn't budge. "Garek will leave, Robbie. You don't need a gun."

"Who said I want him to leave? Caspar and I came up with a better idea." His gaze on Garek, Robbie ground a dirt clod from the sculpture under his heel. "My aim has improved since the business with Rafe, *perro.* You better do what I tell you, or you'll be sorry."

"What is it you want?"

"You're going to marry Ellie," Robbie said deliberately. "My friend Caspar here is an ordained minister."

Caspar gave a little wave from the bedroom.

"Robbie!" Ellie was horrified. "Are you insane?" She sniffed the air, then looked at him suspiciously. "Were you smoking something while you were in the bedroom?"

"No way," Robbie said. "I'm clean. I just want your baby to have a daddy."

Ellie felt, rather than saw, Garek turn to stare at her. Her cheeks burned, but she didn't look away from her cousin. "Robbie, I told you before I'm *not* pregnant. Put that gun down right now—" She started forward, only to stop when Garek put his arm around her shoulders. She glanced up at him and received a shock. In spite of his cool facade, a muscle ticced in his jaw, and fury blazed in his eyes. A sick feeling of dread rose inside her.

"Very well," he said to Robbie. "Let's hurry up and get this over with, then."

Triumph flashed in Robbie's eyes. Keeping the gun trained on Garek, he stepped aside so Caspar could emerge from the room. The tall thin man approached the happy couple and opened a white leather prayer book.

"Dearly beloved…" he proclaimed.

Ellie's body jerked in silent protest. The arm around her shoulders tightened.

"Better to play along," Garek said to her under cover of Caspar's booming voice, "than to risk someone getting hurt. We can deal with it afterward."

"No," she said stubbornly. "Robbie, I refuse to go

through with this ceremony. What are you going to do about it? Shoot me?"

His big brown eyes took on a wounded look. "You know I would never hurt you, Ellie," he said indignantly. "I would just have to shoot your boyfriend."

"That's not funny, Robbie." She knew he didn't really mean it. But then he hadn't really meant to shoot Rafe, either. Could she ever forgive herself if he accidentally hurt Garek?

When she didn't say anything for a few seconds, Caspar cleared his throat. "Do you, Garek, take this woman…"

"This is ridiculous!" she burst out. "It's completely illegal. Don't we have to have blood tests or something?"

Caspar shook his head. "The law is much more lenient nowadays. Blood tests aren't required."

"But what about a license? We have to have a license!"

"Don't worry," Caspar informed her. "I can print a blank one off the Internet. They're good in any state."

As Caspar proceeded with the ceremony, Ellie glanced despairingly at Garek, hoping for some help.

He was watching her with a cynical twist to his mouth that made her stiffen. How dare he look at her like that? As if…as if he thought she *wanted* to marry him.

Garek made his responses in a calm, cool voice that caused her to grit her teeth. She had to choke out the words.

"I now pronounce you husband and wife," Caspar said.

"Congratulations," Robbie said, beaming at the two of them over the top of his gun.

"Thanks," Garek said, his voice full of sarcasm. "We appreciate your…good wishes. You two can leave now. My…*wife* and I would like to be alone."

Robbie shook his head. "No way. We've got to make sure this marriage starts off right."

Ellie didn't know what he was talking about and at this point she didn't care. She felt completely drained. This night that she'd so looked forward to had turned into a nightmare. The only good thing about it was that it couldn't possibly get any worse….

"You two need a wedding night." Robbie sat down on a chair and used the gun to motion the couple toward Ellie's bedroom. "And I'm going to make sure you get it."

Inside the bedroom, the newlyweds stared at each other for a long moment.

Ellie broke the silence first. "So what do we do now?"

He shrugged. "Go to bed." He sat down on the mattress and lay back, watching her. "I hope you don't snore."

She stared at him. "You've got to be joking."

"No, I'm not. I'm a light sleeper and snoring keeps me awake—"

"Not about *that*." She waved her hand impatiently. "I mean about spending the night here. Together."

He put his hands behind his head. "I don't see that we have much choice."

"Are you crazy? We do have a choice. We can wait until Robbie falls asleep. Or we can try to go through the window—"

"Too dangerous. I have no desire to risk waking your trigger-happy cousin, or to get shot in the rear as I try to shimmy out the window." He dismissed her plans with a yawn, then patted the mattress beside him. "Come to bed…*wife*."

Ellie couldn't stop staring at him. Was he insane? She

knew he was angry. Why wasn't he yelling at her? Why was he pretending this marriage was real? "Garek, stop fooling around."

"Who's fooling?" In one swift, graceful motion, he rose to his feet and crossed the room to where she still stood by the door. He put his hands on the wooden panel on either side of her head and bent down to touch his mouth lightly to hers. "We have all night—let's make the most of it."

His mouth closed over hers, and she forgot to think. The attraction that she'd tried to deny flared up immediately, swamping her brain with Technicolor emotions, flooding her body with fluorescent sensations.

She responded blindly, instinctively. His arms came around her, hers curled around his neck. His grip on her tightened; then suddenly, he lifted her and carried her across the room.

He laid her gently on the bed, still kissing her, pulling off his coat and shirt and quickly unbuttoning her blouse. His warm hand cupped the curve of her breast.

Air grated in her lungs. She felt as though she were on fire. His kiss wasn't gentle. It wasn't tentative or kind or respectful. Instead, it was hungry, carnal, overwhelming, unstoppable. His mouth pulled on hers, as if trying to suck the very soul out of her, so he could take possession of it, take possession of her....

She broke away, gasping for air. "Stop," she panted. "We can't do this..."

He kissed the line of her throat, down to the curves of her lace-covered breasts. His fingers undid the button of her skirt, and eased down the zipper, spreading the fabric to expose a scrap of silk and a line of lace.

"Why not? You got what you wanted, didn't you? Marriage to Chicago's Most Eligible Bachelor…"

The sarcasm in his voice broke through the haze threatening to envelope her. What was he talking about? Did the conceited jerk really think she wanted this? That she wanted to marry *him*, a man who was using her to punish his sister?

She pushed at his shoulders.

He resisted. His fingers teased under the line of lace, pausing to splay across the indentation between her hip and abdomen, before drifting lower still…

Flattening her palms against his chest, she shoved harder.

With a curse, he rolled away. She scrambled onto her knees, ready to flee the bed if he made any move toward her. But he didn't. He lay there, his breathing harsh, his arm thrown over his eyes. His whole aspect was one of pain.

The frantic racing of her heart slowed. Uncertainty trickled through her. She touched his arm tentatively. "Garek?"

He stiffened under her touch. He lowered his arm and looked at her, his eyes cold and hard. "Next time you plan to trap a man into marriage," he said, his voice like shards of glass, "make sure you have the guts to go through with it."

Ellie's hand fell to her side. "What are you talking about?"

He stood up and gestured toward the door and where her cousin had positioned himself outside. "The shotgun wedding. The reluctant bride. I thought I'd seen every trick in the book when it came to women trying to ensnare me, but this one, I admit, was brilliant." He looked down at her, his gaze traveling from her face to her chest. "You're one hot little witch when you want to be."

Realizing her blouse was hanging open, she flushed and pulled the edges together. Then she paled. "Surely you don't think I *planned* this. You're the one that barged in here—"

"Yeah, after you left that message that ensured that I would—I was actually feeling guilty for having used you—for misjudging you. But I got it right the first time, didn't I? You're a greedy, manipulative little gold digger, out to make a quick buck."

"I don't care about your money—"

"It's a little late for the innocent act. You set me up. You don't really expect me to believe that your witless cousin came up with this marriage idea on his own? Or that the presence of Caspar, the friendly minister, was merely a coincidence? Oh, and let's not forget the icing on the wedding cake—you, the *pregnant* bride. Tell me something—are you really pregnant? Did some guy knock you up and you decided to pass the baby off as mine? Or was the whole thing a story you invented to get your cousin and his friend to go along with your plan?"

Her face felt frozen. "You…you conceited ass. This whole mess is *your* fault. None of this would have happened if you hadn't decided to play such a nasty trick on your sister. Even if I *were* pregnant, I would never marry you. I wouldn't marry you for all the sculptures in the Metropolitan. I wouldn't marry you for all the paintings in the Louvre. I wouldn't marry you—"

"I get the idea. If you don't mind, I'm going to get some sleep. I have to work tomorrow."

She hated the indifference of his tone. She hated

even more that she couldn't match it—her voice sounded slightly shrill as she asked, "But where are you going to sleep?"

"In the bed, of course." He picked up the pillow and punched it.

"This is *my* bed."

"I'm willing to share. Your virtue is safe with me."

She glared at him. "You can sleep on the floor."

"I'm not that chivalrous. *You* sleep on the floor."

She watched with fury and dismay as he turned back the hand-stitched quilt Aunt Alma had made and sat down to shuck off his shoes. The jerk. The cad. The—

His hands went to the buckle of his belt.

Her cheeks burning again, she practically leaped off the bed and stood with her back to him. A few seconds later she heard the rustle of sheets and the click of the light. The room went dark.

Ellie hesitated, trying to decide what to do. She was *not* going to share a bed with him. But the only other option was the bare wooden planks of the floor.

She considered marching out into the living room and taking the couch. She knew Robbie wouldn't stop her. The only problem was, he would probably come in and shoot Garek. Oh, she didn't think he would kill him—at least not intentionally. But it would be just like Robbie to accidentally shoot Garek in the foot or the hand. Or the rear....

She glanced at the black silhouette in her bed. For a second, she was tempted to go to the couch and leave Garek to his fate.

She sighed. She couldn't do that. No matter how much she hated Garek, she couldn't allow Robbie to shoot him.

An hour later, though, turning on the hard floor, she wasn't so sure. She was so cold, her bones ached with it. She couldn't stop shivering. She pulled her knees up to her chest, trying to conserve her body heat. She didn't remember ever being this cold. The clunky furnace must have conked out again. She would probably freeze by morning....

Warm arms suddenly encircled and lifted her. She gave a little squeak, all she was capable of at the moment since she was shivering so badly. "Wh-what are you doing?"

"The chattering of your teeth is keeping me awake," he growled.

"W-well, isn't that just too bad?" She yelped as he dropped her and she hit the mattress. "I would rather freeze to death than share a bed with you," she informed him haughtily.

"If you insist. At least you'll save me the cost of a lawyer to dissolve this marriage. Just do it quietly."

Outraged, she sat up and glared through the dark at him. Suddenly, she was determined *not* to freeze to death. She wouldn't give him the satisfaction.

Not to mention the warmth of the bed was so heavenly, she didn't think she could get up if she wanted to.

Carefully, she eased herself, still fully clothed, between the blanket and the sheet, trying to ignore the black bulk sprawled beside her in the spot on the mattress where she usually slept.

"You know," he drawled, "you might have grounds to claim the marriage is valid if we consummate it—"

"No, thank you!" she snapped.

He laughed softly, sardonically.

She turned on her side and scooted to the very edge of the mattress.

If he made *one move* toward her, she would shoot him herself.

* * *

Ellie woke up slowly, aware that something was different than usual. Her nose twitched. What was that smell? It wasn't unpleasant exactly. It was more earthy. Musky. Masculine…

Her eyes flew open.

A brawny shoulder was only a few inches away from her own. Instinctively, she pulled away, then, as Garek stirred and rolled over, she grew still, holding her breath.

He didn't wake up, however, and she stared at him. In the clear light filtering through the blinds, she could see every detail. A cowlick spiked up on top of his head. His hair grew back from his wide forehead in a straight line. He frowned, even in his sleep, a crease showing between his eyebrows. He had short, dark lashes, a reasonably well-shaped nose and ears that stuck out slightly, giving him an almost boyish look. The boyishness was instantly belied, however, by the dark shadow of beard and mustache, and the clean line of his upper lip and the full, amazingly sensual curve of his lower lip.

Her chest began to hurt. Two days ago, she'd thought he was someone special. Two days ago, she might have welcomed last night's crazy ceremony—only without the gun.

How could she have been so stupid?

But there was no point in crying. She'd cried over Rafe. She wasn't going to cry over Garek Wisnewski.

She climbed out of the bed. Straightening her spine and smoothing her creased and twisted skirt as best she could, she went to the door and peeked out.

No gun-wielding madmen lurked in the hall.

She checked the other bedroom but saw no sign of

Robbie or his friend. They must have decided to make themselves scarce.

Wisely, thought Ellie as she went into the kitchen and started some coffee. She was going to kill Robbie when she got her hands on him….

A sound made her turn. Garek stood in the doorway, buttoning his shirt, his coat over his arm. His hair was wet and slicked back, but dark stubble still covered his jaw.

"Your cousin decided not to stay for the rest of the honeymoon?"

Ellie turned away from the sardonic tone in Garek's voice. Opening a drawer, she stared down at the contents. She wouldn't let him bait her, she told herself grimly. She'd done nothing wrong. "Would you like some coffee?"

"How wifely you sound."

Closing the drawer with a small bang, she turned to face him. Then paused. She took a deep breath. "Look, I'm sorry about what happened. Robbie is sometimes a bit…impulsive. But he means well."

"I'm sure Al Capone and Bonnie and Clyde had pure motives, also."

She clenched her jaw until the filling in her back molar ached. "I'm sorry you were forced to spend the night here, but no harm done, right?" She pasted a smile on her face. "As you said, the marriage wasn't valid."

He didn't smile back. If anything, the angles of his face grew harsher. "My lawyer will take care of any legalities involved. I am instructing him, however, not to give you a single penny."

"Fine," she said. "I don't want anything from you."

His eyes narrowed. "You really expect me to believe that you're not going to make some claim against me?"

"I don't care what you believe, but that's the truth."

"That's good," he said. "Because you're not getting anything."

"Yes, you already said that." She was tired of his accusations, his suspicion. She stalked out of the kitchen, stepped to the front door and opened it, letting in a blast of cold air. Turning, she spoke across the small space to where he stood in the kitchen doorway watching her. "You better go now and get your lawyer working on it right away."

Garek frowned as he approached her. She played the innocent so well. But he wasn't falling for it this time. "Very well. My lawyer will be in touch with you." He pulled on his coat and gloves. "I'm going to make certain that you're prosecuted for attempted fraud."

"Fine!" she said through gritted teeth. "Just go!"

Garek stepped toward the door. "My lawyer will also make certain that your lunatic cousin is sent back to jail—"

"Robbie?" For the first time Garek saw a crack in her facade. She shut the door abruptly. "You can't do that. Robbie didn't mean any harm—"

"Holding a gun on a person usually qualifies as intending harm. He belongs in prison—"

"He just needs a chance," she said fiercely. "If you do anything to hurt Robbie, I'll…I'll tell the whole story about our marriage to the tabloids."

So *that* was how she intended to turn the situation to her advantage. He'd known she must have some plan up her sleeve. His anger, which had begun to fade, flared up to new heights. "Do whatever the hell you like," he snarled. "I really don't give a damn."

He opened the door and strode out of the apartment. Head bent against the cold wind, he silently cursed himself for believing, just for a moment, that she was as innocent as she looked.

Chapter Ten

Garek worked long, hard hours the next week. Other than giving his lawyer a terse explanation and an even terser set of instructions, he did not think of Eleanor Hernandez at all—except, perhaps, when he chanced to glance at the abstract painting hanging on his wall. Then he couldn't quite control the acid burn in his stomach.

He was searching his desk drawer for a roll of antacids as he talked on the phone to his production manager late Friday afternoon, when the door opened and Larry Larson, head of the legal department for Wisnewski Industries, entered the office.

"Let me get back to you, Ed." Garek hung up the phone, his gaze on Larry's face. "Well?"

"I've got good news and bad news." Larry sat down, carefully positioning the fall of his jacket as he seated himself. He had a fondness for expensive suits and a tendency to comb his hair across the bald spot on his crown, but he was an excellent lawyer, intelligent and efficient, and Garek knew he could count on him for sound advice.

"Go on," Garek said.

"The good news is that I spoke to several experts and they confirmed what I told you initially—any marriage involving coercion is automatically invalid. Also, after careful research, I've discovered that virtually every state refuses to recognize Internet marriage licenses. Ms. Hernandez will have a very difficult time making any claim against you."

Garek leaned back in his chair, his hard gaze not leaving the lawyer's face. "And the bad news?"

"The bad news—ah." Larry cleared his throat and adjusted his cuff. "The bad news is that coercion can be a difficult thing to prove. She could claim that the two of you married of your own free will. Then it would be her word against yours. Also, one or two states do recognize Internet marriage licenses. Vermont, for example, recognizes just about anything as a marriage. And unfortunately, Caspar Egilbert *is* a legally ordained minister, even though the university he obtained his degree from is somewhat suspect. The unpleasant truth is that although I have no doubt that we would ultimately be successful, I'm afraid Ms. Hernandez could involve us in a very messy, very embarrassing court case and the resulting publicity would not be good for the company. Stockholders want their CEOs to be above reproach these days—"

"I don't care about the damn stockholders." The anger Garek had been controlling all week flared dangerously high. "I'm not paying her one dime—"

"Yes, yes," Larry said hastily, fingering the knot of his tie. "Fortunately, that won't be necessary. If you'll look in this file, you'll see that I've taken care of all the paperwork."

Hard satisfaction replaced the burn in Garek's stomach. He took the thick file from Larry and opened it. Inside on top was a document giving him ownership of the gallery. He picked up a pen. "Did the accountant go over the books?"

"Yes, everything was in order. Although there was one thing that seemed a bit odd...."

Tensing, Garek glanced up. "What?"

"A donation to the Art Institute a few days ago."

"What's so odd about that?"

"The artist was paid five thousand for the work. Coincidentally, a check you'd made out to Ms. Hernandez was cashed the same day...."

Garek's grip tightened on the pen.

"I called the Art Institute and discovered that the donation had been made in *your* name. I asked what exactly the donation was, and the woman said it was a sculpture of a giant..." Larry paused.

"A giant cockroach?" Garek guessed.

Larry's nearly nonexistent eyebrows rose. "You knew about this?"

"Not exactly." Narrowing his eyes, Garek signed the deed and set it aside. He stared down at the next paper, a document stating that one Eleanor Hernandez relinquished all claims on him. "This is already signed," Garek observed.

"Yes," Larry said, his satisfaction evident. "I spoke to her this morning."

"Did she give you any trouble?"

"Surprisingly, no. I think she realized she was beat. She read through the waiver and the annulment papers, then signed them both. She did ask me to remind you what she'd said about her cousin, though."

"Ah, yes. Her cousin." Garek set Ellie's waiver aside and glanced at the next document—a statement against Robbie. Phrases like *assault with a deadly weapon* and *criminal confinement* leaped out at him.

He'd been too furious about the whole shotgun marriage and her threat to sell her story to the tabloids to think about Eleanor Hernandez very clearly. All he'd thought of this last week were ways to squash her gallery, her cousin and—most especially—her.

But now, something nagged at him, something that had been niggling at the back of his brain all week.

She'd been extremely upset when the reporter had taken a picture of Garek and her, insisting that he go after the man and get the film. She'd even refused to be interviewed when it could have helped her precious gallery. She'd claimed she wanted the attention focused on the artists and their work, but the more he thought about it, the more certain he was that she found the idea of appearing in a tabloid as distasteful as he did.

Garek frowned.

If she was trying to blackmail him, she wasn't doing a very good job of it. She should have threatened to go to the tabloids if he didn't give her money—not to save her cousin. If money was what she was after, she should have cashed that five-thousand-dollar check weeks ago, not squandered it on a ridiculous donation to the Art Institute, a donation designed to…what? Embarrass him? Make some point?

If she wanted to make any kind of claim on him at all, she should have refused to sign these papers. She should have let him make love to her that night, encouraged him to consummate their "marriage"….

It didn't make any sense. *She* didn't make any sense—

"Ahem."

Garek looked up to see Larry watching him. The lawyer pointed to the line at the bottom of the complaint. "You just need to sign there—"

Garek pushed the paper aside. "I've changed my mind. I'm not going to have Roberto Hernandez arrested. I want to leave him out of this."

Larry's mouth fell open. "But why?"

"I don't want to have it on public record that I was coerced into marriage at gunpoint."

Lines formed on the lawyer's forehead. "Since when have you cared what anyone thinks?"

Garek's eyebrows lifted. "You should be happy—you're always telling me I should worry about it."

Larry's frown deepened. "You can't let this man off. He's a menace, a danger to society—"

"You're afraid he'll go all over town forcing men to marry his cousin?" Garek asked sardonically. "Somehow, I'm not too concerned."

"I don't think it's wise," Larry said unhappily. "Without the legal complaint, it will be easier for Ms. Hernandez to claim that you weren't coerced."

"She's already signed away all claims."

"That doesn't mean she couldn't change her mind. If she gets herself a sharp lawyer, she could—"

"I'm willing to take that chance," Garek interrupted. "I've made my decision."

"Very well," Larry said, his voice as stiff as the hair covering his bald spot. "If you'll just sign the annulment papers, I'll go."

Garek glanced down at the last document, then set it aside also. "I have a meeting shortly. I'll do it later."

"All you have to do is sign it."

"I want to look it over," Garek said coldly. He turned his attention to some other papers. Without looking at his lawyer, he said, "That will be all, Larry."

When Garek heard the door close, he looked up. He stared at nothing in particular for several seconds. Then, slowly, he picked up the annulment papers again. He flipped to the back page where Ellie had signed the document.

He studied her signature for a long moment—the delicate pen strokes, the looping "E" in "Eleanor," the elegant "H" in "Hernandez."

An image flashed through his head of the morning he'd woken in Ellie's apartment. He'd immediately been aware that something was wrong—the pillowcase under his cheek was cheap cotton instead of silk, cold air stung the parts of his skin not covered by a heavy, fluffy comforter, and there was a heady scent nearby—one that made his body harden instantly. He'd opened his eyes slowly.

He'd seen dark tousled curls; long, black lashes lying heavily on delicately flushed cheeks; and red, soft lips, slightly parted, inviting him to lean over and kiss her....

He'd closed his eyes again and waited until she got up and left the room. Only then had he risen and dressed. But instead of leaving immediately, he'd looked around her room, noticing the antique iron bed frame and old-fashioned quilt that contrasted oddly with the abstract paintings hanging on the wall. On the white-washed dresser was a small oval frame with a picture of two people. The man, blond with blue eyes, had a cheerful smile. The woman had dark hair and eyes and her face was solemn, a few lines giving her a more care-worn expression than the man. The two of them hadn't been looking at each other, but there was an indefinable aura about them, something about the way the man's hand held the woman's arm so tenderly and the way the woman tilted her head toward the man, that had made Garek stare at the picture for a long, long time....

Garek set the annulment papers down on his desk. Closing the file, he picked up the phone and dialed.

Chapter Eleven

She wouldn't talk to him.

Garek grew more and more annoyed as the day wore on and Ellie didn't answer the phone or return his calls. He went to the gallery, but Tom, the timid artist, told him in a quaking voice that she wasn't going to be in that day—or tomorrow, either. He went to her apartment, but either she wasn't home, or she refused to answer the door.

By the next day, he was at the end of his patience. He called and left a message on her answering machine.

"If you want to keep your job at Vogel's, you'd better present yourself at my office at 3:00 p.m. sharp this afternoon."

She called several times after that, but Garek told Mrs. Grist not to put the calls through.

That afternoon, at precisely three o'clock, she stalked into his office, quivering with indignation.

"What are you up to now?" Stopping by the leather

chair in front of his desk, Ellie glared at Garek. "Are you going to try to talk Mr. Vogel into firing me? He won't listen to you. He'll believe me—"

"I won't be talking to Vogel anymore at all." Garek stood up slowly. He looked more controlled than usual, his tie straight, his hair neatly combed, his jacket lying smoothly across his shoulders. His expression was harder and more remote than ever. "I just purchased the gallery from him."

Ellie grew very still, staring into his eyes. Surrounded by short, black lashes, they were as gray as the sky outside, as cold as the water in Lake Michigan.

She swallowed, even that small movement difficult and painful. "I don't believe you," she whispered. "Mr. Vogel would have told me."

But even as she spoke the words, Ellie knew they weren't necessarily true. Al Vogel was growing increasingly frail and forgetful—and although she hadn't wanted to admit it to herself, she'd known he would have to sell the gallery soon.

"Ask him."

Ellie felt stunned. Garek might be lying—but she doubted it. What would be the point? The office had seemed warm when she first came in, but now she felt cold in spite of her thick, cable-knit sweater. She pressed her forearm against her middle, against the queasiness in her stomach. The gallery—*her* gallery—purchased by Garek Wisnewski. She was at his mercy—as was everyone Vogel's supported.

And didn't he know it. He stood there behind his enormous desk, surrounded by his fancy furniture, like a king waiting to hear a penitent's plea. He was waiting for her to apologize, she realized. Waiting for her to beg for mercy. Her nails dug into the thick yarn of her sweater. As if she would *ever* give him that satisfaction.

"So," she said proudly, pressing her forearm more tightly against her roiling stomach. "Did you summon me here to fire me? Or to tell me you're closing the gallery? Or just to gloat?"

"All very attractive options, but first I want to ask you about something else. I understand you donated a certain sculpture to the Art Institute. In my name."

It had seemed like a good idea at the time. Although now, in retrospect…

But it was too late for caution, too late for regrets.

She lifted her chin. "Yes, I *did* give Bertrice's sculpture to the museum. I told them there was only one condition—they had to display your name prominently. Everyone who goes to the museum will look at that cockroach, then look at the name Garek Wisnewski. I'm sure that everyone who knows you will immediately understand the connection—"

"You may be right," he said in a disgustingly calm voice. "Tell me something—was it worth five thousand dollars?"

"It was worth ten times that amount!" She shivered, but from rage now, not cold. "I know this is beyond your comprehension, but I don't want your money, I never did! I only took that five thousand dollars because you were so rude. But now I'm glad I took it because it helped Bertrice, and I'm glad that out of all the misery you've caused, at least one person benefited, and I'm glad that the whole world can see now what an insect you really are—"

"Are you finished?"

She gripped the back of the leather chair. "Yes. I am.

Will you at least wait until I can find another place to take the art before you close Vogel's?"

"I'm not closing the gallery."

She thought she must have misheard him. "What did you say?"

"I want the gallery to stay open—and I want you to continue to run it."

Tense and disbelieving, she stared at him. "Why?"

"Maybe I'm afraid you'll sell your story about our marriage to the tabloids."

"I said I was only going to do that if you turned Robbie in," she pointed out.

"Are you saying that I can close the gallery and not worry about reprisals?"

"Yes. I mean, no…that is—"

"Would you go out to dinner with me?"

He couldn't be serious. And yet, his eyes were dark and intent, his mouth a straight, unsmiling line.

"I'm surprised you'd want to go out with a 'criminal' like me," she said, trying to gather her scattered wits.

"I'm making an exception in your case."

"Why?"

"Does there have to be a reason?"

"Yes," she said decisively. "There does."

He put his hands in his pockets. "I suppose I thought we could be…friends."

"Friends?" she repeated in disbelief. After using her, insulting her and accusing her of trying to trap him into marriage, he wanted to be *friends?* She didn't think so. "No, thank you," she said coldly. "I'm very particular about my friends."

He didn't seem offended by her rudeness. "I can be a very good friend."

"What's that supposed to mean?"

"I can put a lot more money into the art foundation. I can move your gallery to the fashionable part of town. I can—"

"Are you trying to bribe me into going out with you?" she asked.

"No, of course not."

"That's good. Because the answer is still no."

His gaze was inscrutable. "The silent auction Stacy Hatfield arranged is this Saturday at my sister's."

"So?"

"You have to be there. It's business."

"I'm sure Stacy can handle it."

"It's imperative that you be present. Donors like to see the people involved before they give money."

"They can see your sister and you."

His eyes narrowed. "I can also be a very bad enemy."

She gaped at him. "Are you *threatening* me now?"

"I'm only trying to ensure the foundation is a success," he said smoothly. "I've invested a lot of money in it."

"Yeah, right. I suppose I have no choice, then." She glared at him. "Tell me, do you always have to black-mail women into a date?"

"No," he said grimly. "You're the first."

"You should never have made me go through with this," Doreen Tarrington hissed at Garek as she smiled and nodded at a couple helping themselves to shrimp and prosciutto appetizers. "It's going to be a disaster."

"Perhaps. Perhaps not," Garek drawled in a bored tone. His sister had been nagging at him ever since he'd ordered her to go ahead with the dinner party. She'd whined and complained and dragged her size-ten feet, but in the end, when faced with the prospect of paying the cost of her next face-lift herself, she'd reluctantly agreed.

"I warn you, Garek," Doreen said in threatening accents, "if that tawdry little girlfriend of yours or her cartoon-character friend embarrass me in front of my friends I will never speak to you again."

Garek thought of several unkind responses, but managed to restrain himself. His object wasn't to be at odds with his sister all evening. "I'm sure Ellie and Caspar will behave in a perfectly normal manner," he responded, his gaze turning to the couple in question.

A slight frown creased his forehead. He hadn't expected Ellie to bring Caspar along. Apparently, Stacy Hatfield had told Ellie to choose an artist for the guests to meet. That would have been fine—if Ellie had picked just about anyone other than Roberto's friend.

Originally, when Garek's only purpose was to punish his sister, he would have been delighted by Caspar's presence. Now, he only wanted everything to go smoothly.

Looking at Caspar's gangly form and Ellie's overly bright smile and stiff back, he began to suspect that he'd made a few miscalculations…

Suddenly, Ellie turned her head and her gaze met his. Even across the crowded room, he could see the way her eyes flashed.

The dinner bell rang. She looked away and began to move with the other guests toward the dining room.

Garek followed, aware of a slight sense of trepidation.

Ellie didn't want to be there. She didn't want to be in this ugly, overly ornate house, with its fussy details and chairs and sofas that seemed to shout, "We are expensive pieces of furniture!" She did not want to talk and try to be polite to the snobbish Mrs. Tarrington whose nose quivered every time she came near and who seemed to regard her like an insect she'd found in her salad. And, most of all, she didn't want to be sitting in this dining room, eating bouillabaisse, forced to look at Garek Wisnewski every time she raised her gaze from her soup.

She glared across the table at him, but he didn't appear to notice, so deep in conversation was he with Amber Bellair, his blond ex-girlfriend. Amber's "little black dress" made Ellie's simple blue frock look like something from a thrift store—which, in fact, it was.

Garek, in his dark suit that fit snugly across his shoulders, made the perfect companion for the blonde—although the garish colors of the tie Ellie had given him for his birthday clashed horribly with Amber's simple elegance. Why was he wearing it? To remind Ellie how naive and stupid she'd been when she'd given it to him?

She couldn't imagine what he hoped to gain by this whole charade. She didn't believe for a second his sorry excuse that he just wanted to be "friends." More likely he wanted to continue with his plan to annoy his sister.

Well, she had no intention of cooperating. No matter how rude Mrs. Tarrington was.

Ellie looked a little anxiously at Caspar, who was sitting at the opposite end of the table. She'd originally intended to bring one of the gallery artists, but she'd felt obliged to warn them that the hostess did not care for contemporary art, and in fact was openly hostile toward it. They'd all refused to attend—no big surprise there. Caspar, however, had begged to come, saying that it was his big chance to make contact with some people who might buy his work. She'd been so angry at Garek, she'd finally agreed, thinking that the whole evening would be a farce, anyway. She'd thought that Garek and Doreen would probably like the ex-convict's vapid paintings.

But now Ellie regretted her temper. She hated to subject any artist—however questionable his talent—to Garek's snobbish sister. Fortunately, Caspar seemed oblivious to Doreen's gibes, and the other guests weren't as bad as Ellie had expected. Most of them, in contrast to their hostess, were very friendly. In fact, many were genuinely interested in art, and one or two were even extraordinarily knowledgeable.

But then there were a few…

Brandon Carlyle, a pompous, middle-aged lawyer, was presently telling everyone about his favorite restaurant.

"There's a place at the foot of the Swiss Alps," he droned at a peculiarly slow speed, "that I highly recommend. The food is all of the finest quality. They serve blue oxtail soup seasoned and cooked to perfection. I've had blue oxtail soup in New York and in Paris, but in my opinion, it's not quite as good."

"Oh, come on, Brandon." Sam Kroner, a man in his middle thirties with blond hair and smiling blue eyes, leaned forward to address the other man. "The *best* food is always the food you catch yourself. When Bonnie and I were on vacation in Alaska, we caught a trout that was the best I've ever tasted. Isn't that right, BonBon?"

Sam's wife nodded. "The only bad part was cleaning it—"

"The best fish *I* ever had was in Hawaii," Doreen interrupted, her loud voice carrying clearly to where Ellie sat halfway down the table. "It was absolutely delicious. Remember, Amber? You and Garek had dinner at that little place in Honolulu once, I believe."

"Yes, I remember. It was good. *Very* good."

Amber looked at Garek in a way that made Ellie think the blonde wasn't just talking about the fish.

"Tell us, Ms. Hernandez," Doreen went on. "What is *your* favorite restaurant?"

Ellie looked up and glanced at the faces around the table. Everyone seemed to be staring at her. "The Taco Palace," she said. "It has the best fish tacos you can imagine."

Sarah Carlyle laughed, causing some soup to drip from her spoon onto her white dress. Still smiling, she dabbed at the greenish stain with her napkin. "The Taco Palace? I've never heard of it. But I love fish tacos. Where is it?"

"Near the corner of Twenty-fifth and Kedzie in Little Village."

"I like Mexican food, too," Sam said. "Do they make enchiladas?"

"The best," Ellie assured him. "Although I have to warn you, I may be a little biased. My uncle owns the place."

Peter Branwell, who owned a national chain of restaurants, looked up from his soup. "Your uncle owns the Taco Palace? I've heard of it—it has an excellent reputation for inexpensive, high-quality food. Has your uncle ever thought of franchising?"

"No, he prefers to keep the restaurant family-owned and operated."

Doreen gave a tinkling laugh. "Family-owned and operated? You make it sound as if you've actually worked there."

Ellie met her gaze calmly. "I have. As a waitress."

"A waitress?" Doreen waved at the maid to remove the soup bowls. "Not a profession most people would aspire to. But perhaps you come from a long line of waitresses?"

"No, my mother cleaned houses."

"Dear me. And your father?"

A rueful smile curved Ellie's lips. "Poor Papa. He was most often unemployed, I'm afraid. His last job was as a used-car salesman."

"I've bought used cars for the last twenty years," Sam commented as the maid set a dessert plate in front of him. "Maybe I bought one from your father. Hernandez… Hmm, it doesn't ring a bell. What was his first name?"

"I doubt you knew him—we lived in Philadelphia." Ellie reached toward the two forks above her plate. She hesitated, then picked up one and took a bite of her dessert. "Mmm, cherries jubilee, my favorite."

"Ahem." Doreen cleared her throat delicately and pointedly picked up another fork. "After hearing about your background, I can see why some of the finer aspects of etiquette must be bewildering to you."

Ellie switched forks and smiled sweetly. "Oh, no, not at all. My mother taught me that truly good manners mean making other people comfortable."

Ellie thought she saw Garek smile, but then he covered his mouth with his hand and coughed. "It's time to proceed with the silent auction," he said, rising to his feet. "We have a special item this evening, from Vogel's Gallery. The artist, Caspar Egilbert, will tell you about it. Caspar?"

Caspar, who'd been deep in conversation with the Palermos at the other end of the table, stood also, pushing his lank brown hair back from his face. The motion caused the sleeves of his ill-fitting brown suit to hike up, exposing his bony wrists. He ambled over to the easel. "I created this painting especially for this occasion. It is symbolic of the many influences in my life, and my love and appreciation for my mother." He whipped off the covering, revealing...breasts.

Hundreds of them.

Pointy, sagging and siliconed breasts. Brown, pink and one pair of blue breasts. Lopsided, tattooed and hairy breasts. Breasts with nipples that, through some trick of perspective, always seemed to be pointing directly at the viewer no matter where he or she stood— or sat.

Mrs. Branwell's fork clattered onto her plate. Her husband leaned forward and craned his neck to get a better look. Amber folded her arms over her chest. Doreen emitted an odd, muffled noise.

Garek burst out laughing.

"I'm glad you found the evening so amusing," Ellie said several hours later as Garek was driving her home. "I don't think your sister did. But that was your intention, wasn't it?"

"At first, perhaps," he admitted. "What about you? Did you enjoy yourself?"

"It could have been worse," she said, not very graciously. But she didn't want to admit that she *had* had a good time. After Garek burst into laughter, everyone had seemed to loosen up. The silent auction had gone well, with George Palermo and Sam Kroner getting into a bidding war over Caspar's painting. Through it all, Ellie had chatted with the guests. Amber had left early,

but everyone else had appeared to enjoy themselves—
everyone except Doreen.

Looking stiff and mortified, Doreen Tarrington had
barely spoken a word to anyone the remainder of the
evening. Unfortunately, the one person she did speak to
was Ellie. The older woman pulled her aside at one
point to "warn" her about Garek. He had committed numerous sins, according to his sister, including neglect-
ing his duty to his family and his position in the
community, as well as cheating her out of her fair share
of their father's company.

Garek turned the car onto Ellie's street and parked
under a streetlight. It provided dim illumination through
the sleet-filled night, but enough that she could see Garek's serious expression as he turned to her.

"I apologize for Doreen," he said quietly.

His words surprised her. "You don't have to. She
didn't bother me."

He shot a skeptical glance at her. "Oh? You didn't
mind being interrogated about your family, having your
manners attacked and being cold-shouldered by your
hostess?"

"Not really. I feel sorry for your sister."

"*Sorry* for her? What on earth for?"

"I see a sad and lonely woman who is trying very
hard to buy her place in life. She doesn't seem to understand that money can't make her happy."

He stared at her. "You honestly think someone with
no money can be as happy as someone with a large
bank account?"

Ellie thought about some of the hardships she'd experienced since coming to Chicago—working twelve-
and fourteen-hour days; eating nothing but rice and

beans in order to make her rent payment; and the sick feeling in the pit of her stomach at the end of every month when she balanced the gallery's books and saw the steadily increasing red ink. "I suppose money can smooth the way," she admitted. "But haven't you ever noticed that no matter how much people have, they always want more? If they make ten thousand dollars, they want thirty thousand dollars. If they make a hundred thousand dollars, they want a hundred and fifty thousand dollars. They're never satisfied with what they have."

He stared at her with an odd expression she couldn't quite define. She expected him to argue with her, to ridicule her for being naive and simplistic.

"It's kind of you to say Doreen didn't bother you," he said, directing his gaze toward the sleet-battered windshield. "But I know that's not true. I saw how nervous you were."

She glanced at him in surprise. What was he talking about? She hadn't been nervous. Angry, maybe, but not nervous. "Did I seem nervous?"

"Yes, you did." He turned his gaze back to her, watching her closely. "I could tell, because in all the time I've known you, as many restaurants as I've taken you to, I've never seen you use the wrong fork before."

"Oh!" Her eyes skittered away, then returned to his. She smiled a little ruefully. "Well, maybe I did egg your sister on a bit. I really shouldn't have."

He didn't say anything else. He got out of the car into the raging sleet and wind. He opened her door for her and ran with her up to her apartment. Sheltered somewhat by the roof, he took her hand. "Will you go to dinner with me tomorrow night?"

She stared at the large hand enveloping hers. Did he really think she could ignore everything that he'd done? Did he really think they could go on as though none of it had happened?

"No," she said, then braced herself, expecting him to argue or try to kiss her.

Instead, he gazed down at her for a long moment, a slight frown between his brows. Suddenly, he raised her hand to his lips and lightly kissed the back of her glove.

Then, without a word, he left, leaving her feeling angry, upset…and strangely confused.

Garek returned to his sister's house to find her pacing the marble tile of the entry hall.

"There you are!" she greeted him accusingly. "I'm surprised you didn't stay all night with your little girlfriend."

"Perhaps I should have."

Doreen gave him a sharp look. "What's going on with you and that girl?"

"Nothing. Absolutely nothing."

"You would like there to be, though, wouldn't you?"

"Is this why you asked me to come back here tonight? So you could interrogate me about my relationship with Ellie?"

"Yes…no! I asked you to come here so I could tell you what I think of you, you bastard! I never should have let you talk me into going forward with this—if I hadn't needed that money so desperately…oh! What my friends must have thought!"

"Your friends appeared to enjoy themselves," Garek said coolly.

"No, thanks to your girlfriend and that horrible artist person. When he unveiled that obscene painting…and you! You were no help, laughing the way you did. I was mortified, absolutely mortified. You knew how much this evening meant to me—and yet you couldn't even be bothered to wear a decent tie!"

He glanced down at the scrap of fabric in question. "I'm beginning to like it," he said. "Ellie gave it to me."

"I'm not at all surprised. You cannot be serious about that girl—oh, don't pretend you don't know what I'm talking about. I saw the way you were looking at her all evening. I admit, she's attractive in a low-class sort of way, but she would never fit in. Just look at her family—her mother a house cleaner, her father a used-car salesman, her uncle a taco maker. Who knows what other distasteful details we'll discover about her background?"

At least one more, if his suspicions were correct, Garek thought, remembering the picture of Ellie's parents in her bedroom.

He looked at his sister. If they'd had this conversation yesterday, he would have been furious. But now, after his conversation with Ellie, he could only think of what she'd said. Doreen's face had the smooth, blank look of someone who'd had a face-lift; there were no smile lines by her eyes, only tiny vertical grooves above her upper lip that made her look bitter and dissatisfied. What had made her that way? he wondered. Out loud, he said, "Ellie fit in perfectly tonight."

"She was tolerated, nothing more. And only because my friends are too polite to say anything. You must watch out for this girl. You know she's only interested in your money. Did you see the way she was eyeing the furniture, as if she was assessing its value?"

"You don't know her," Garek said.

"I know her, all right. Her type is obvious. She's the type to get pregnant and trap a man into marriage."

"No, she's the type to have a cousin who forces her to marry a man at gunpoint."

Doreen's mouth dropped open. "What are you talking about?"

A glimmer of a smile curved Garek's mouth at the sight of Doreen's aghast look. "I'm saying, sister, dear, your warning is too late. Ellie and I are already married."

Chapter Twelve

Ellie looked at the giraffe, wishing she could wring Garek's neck until he looked like a twin of the penned animal in front of her. "Why haven't you signed the annulment papers?" she asked, turning her gaze back to the aggravating creature next to her.

He shrugged and led her to the next enclosure, not responding to her question—another bad habit of his, she thought darkly. When she'd called his office this morning and demanded to speak to him, his assistant had put her on hold, then come back on the line saying Garek was too busy to talk right now, but he'd be glad to meet her at lunchtime at any spot she chose.

"He can talk to me now," Ellie had said sweetly, "or meet me at the zoo."

She hadn't thought the big ape would actually *agree* to her suggestion. She'd been tempted to stand him up—and she probably would have if the matter hadn't been so urgent.

"Why haven't you signed the papers?" she asked again.

"There's been a glitch." He threw a peanut to one of the baboons.

Probably a close relative of his, Ellie thought. "What kind of glitch?"

"Some legal technicality. It should take only a week or two to correct."

"A week or two?" she repeated blankly. For the last couple of days, ever since Doreen Tarrington's dinner party, Ellie had been feeling like she'd fallen down the rabbit hole. First there'd been the influx of customers to the gallery—virtually all of the dinner guests and a multitude of their friends had descended upon Vogel's and purchased at least one art piece. Tom, Carlo and Bertrice were ecstatic.

Ellie should have been delighted too. And she was. Only…she wished Garek wasn't the one largely responsible for the gallery's sudden success. She didn't want to have to be grateful to him. She didn't want to have to even *think* about him. But it was amazingly difficult not to. Especially after the visitor she'd had at the gallery yesterday.

Ellie had just opened, when the bell on the door jingled and a teenager walked in. The tall girl with hostile gray eyes looked vaguely familiar, but it took Ellie a moment to place where she'd seen that thin face and straight brown hair before.

"You're Karen Tarrington, aren't you?" Ellie said.

The girl looked shocked, then suspicious. "How'd you know that?"

"Your uncle showed me a picture of you once."

"He did?" Some emotion flickered in the girl's eyes—but only for a moment. "I didn't know he had one. Mom must have given him my stupid school picture. I'm surprised he didn't throw it away." She glanced disdainfully around the gallery. "What a bunch of junk!"

The girl was as charming as her mother, Ellie thought wryly. "Your family appears to be completely unanimous in that opinion."

Karen stared at a chair covered with beads and bits of glass. "Yeah, Mom's pretty upset. This is going to kill her chance of getting in the Social Register for sure. Are you supposed to sit on this chair?"

Ellie blinked. "No, not really. It's more for decoration. What does Vogel's have to do with your mother and the Social Register?"

"That's why Mom wanted Uncle Garek to start an art foundation. So she could get her name in the Social Register. Uncle Garek thought it was a stupid idea."

For once Ellie had to agree with him. "I'm surprised he didn't refuse her request, then."

"He couldn't. Mom threatened to screw up some business deal he was working on. Uncle Garek was pretty hot under the collar about it."

Appalled, Ellie stared at Karen. "How do you know all this?"

"They were arguing about it on Christmas Eve. They argue a lot. Uncle Garek hates my mom."

"I doubt that's true," Ellie said automatically, then paused. "I think he's just very angry at her for trying to hurt his business," she said more slowly.

Karen shrugged. "Same difference. He hardly ever comes over to our house anymore."

"Did he use to?"

"Yeah, when I was a little kid. He took me to the park and baseball games and stuff like that. Once he took me to the symphony."

"The symphony?"

"Yeah. For my birthday. I was thirteen years old and he bought me a white lace dress with a blue satin bow." Once more, the cynical expression slipped, revealing pure, naked emotion. For a moment, the girl's face was full of such wistfulness, such yearning, that Ellie's breath caught. Then the mask descended once more and Karen sneered. "It was a little kid's dress. I didn't want to wear it, but Mom insisted. I hated it and I hated the stupid symphony. All that lame classical music. Uncle Garek stopped coming by after that. He said he had to work."

Ellie said gently, "That was probably true."

Karen shrugged again. "Yeah, right. At least he buys good presents. He got me a computer for Christmas, and he bought my mom an emerald and ruby necklace. Actually, I thought the necklace was kind of ugly, but Mom didn't care. She always returns everything he gives her for the cash."

Ellie remembered the gaudy necklace with shock. She'd imagined his sister treasuring the ugly jewelry as a sign of his affection—instead, it appeared the woman only cared about the monetary value. Did Garek know? Probably. His anger at his sister obviously went back a long way. But oddly enough, in spite of all the anger and bitterness, she sensed that he really did care about Doreen—

"So what's the deal here?" Karen asked, bending over to look more closely at a fishbone hung in a frame. "Are you my aunt now, or what?"

Ellie froze. "What are you talking about?"

"You and Uncle Garek are married, right? He told Mom last night. She's absolutely livid."

Karen's warning should have prepared Ellie for the phone call she'd received shortly after the girl left—but it hadn't. Remembering the unpleasant conversation, she glared at the South American rodent in the enclosure in front of her, then turned her gaze to its North American counterpart standing next to her. "Did you have to tell your sister?" she asked.

Garek slanted a glance at her. "She gave you a hard time, I take it."

"Did she ever!" Indignation rose in Ellie at the memory. Karen had given her a blatantly skeptical look when Ellie denied the marriage and had left the gallery a few minutes later; Doreen hadn't been nearly so restrained. "The names she called me! And when I finally got her calmed down enough to explain that the ceremony was invalid, that we weren't really married, she called me a liar!"

"Sorry about that," he murmured.

She looked at him suspiciously. "But why did you tell her?"

"It just slipped out."

Ellie gripped the iron railing. "You've never struck me as the type to let things slip."

"Maybe you don't know me as well as you think."

"I know as much as I want to know."

"Are you so sure, Ellie? Why won't you give me a second chance?"

"Why should I?"

"I don't know." He ran his fingers through his hair. "I just know that I don't want you to disappear from my life until we've had a chance to explore this attraction between us."

She glared at him. "Is that what this is all about? Are you still hoping to get me into bed? Well, you won't. I wouldn't go to bed with you if the world was about to end. I wouldn't go to bed with you if the survival of the human species depended on it. I wouldn't go to bed with you if—"

"Okay, okay," he said. "I get the idea."

"I don't think you know how to be friends with a woman."

"You could teach me."

"I don't want to teach you anything." She headed for the door that led out of the Large Mammal House. Freezing-cold wind bit at her face as she started up a winding path. "I've had a revelation. I've realized that sex before marriage is a big mistake. My new philosophy in life is no sex without a wedding ring. What do you think of that?"

"I still want to go out with you."

He must not have heard her. "There would be *no sex*. And no spending lots of money, either. Could you live with that?"

"Yes," he said meekly.

She didn't believe him. He would get tired of a relationship based on nothing more than friendship. She doubted he would last more than a month, if that.

She glanced up at him as they approached an outdoor animal enclosure. "There's a foreign film playing at the college on Saturday and the Azalea Flower Show at Garfield Park the week after that. You can come with me to those," she informed him.

He winced a little, but nodded.

"You understand, no sex," she reiterated.

He nodded again.

Satisfied, she turned to look at the animals in the enclosure.

Two huge polar bears were vigorously mating.

Ellie's eyes widened. She froze. The bears continued their business with the utmost nonchalance.

She sneaked a glance at Garek.

"Unless, of course," he said, completely straight-faced except for a gleam in his eye, "you can't bear to go without."

Chapter Thirteen

"So what do you think?" she asked him one month later during the intermission of the free concert being held at a local college.

Garek eyed the stale doughnuts and cold coffee being sold by some student group in the dingy hallway. He decided against refreshments.

"To be perfectly truthful," he said, turning his gaze back to Ellie, "it's incredibly boring."

He saw the shock register. She stared at him, her lips pursing in an expression of disapproval. But then, her mouth softened, and she laughed. "At least you're honest. But you're spoiled. You're used to easy entertainment. Sometimes you have to make an effort."

"An effort how?"

"You learn about the music, to appreciate it. You imagine a story as it's playing. Or what the music makes you feel. What did you feel with the music we just heard?"

"Sleepy."

She laughed again, but shook her head. "That wasn't much of an effort."

"I save my effort for business."

She looked at him curiously. "Is that the only thing in your life worth exerting yourself for?"

He frowned. A few months ago he would have said yes. Now, he wasn't so sure. "Running a company requires total commitment. Art and music are completely frivolous."

"You're wrong. Art teaches you to observe, to look beyond the surface. Music teaches you to listen, to hear more than what's being said."

A pimply-faced student announced that the music was about to begin again and Ellie didn't say any more, but her words stuck with Garek through the second half of the concert.

Perhaps the business had lost some of its attraction. The company had always demanded a lot of his attention and he'd never minded before. But lately he'd been aware of a vague sense of dissatisfaction. Sometimes he felt as though he was in a dark tunnel, one that was getting narrower and narrower as he proceeded. He couldn't go back, but sometimes he thought that if he kept going forward, the concrete walls would start to press against him, squeezing him until he couldn't breathe….

Maybe that was why he was finding it strangely appealing to go out on weird dates with a woman he wasn't even sleeping with.

She wouldn't let him take her anywhere expensive; they went to museums, lectures and cheap restaurants. It reminded him a little of his childhood, before his father had started the company. Every Saturday, he, his sister and parents had gone to the Navy Pier. Doreen had saved her baby-sitting money and took him for rides on the Ferris wheel and bought him funnel cakes.

He had a lot of good memories of Doreen. She'd been different then; she'd helped their mother cook and clean their small house and flirted with the son of the auto mechanic next door.

After his father started his own business, everything had changed. The business had been wildly successful, and his father had worked long hours and weekends. They rarely saw him after that, but at first Garek really didn't notice. That first year had been like a constant stream of Christmas mornings. His father got a new car, his mother a housekeeper. Garek and his sister received TVs, toys, whatever they wanted. They moved into the fancy Gold Coast neighborhood of Chicago. Only, there hadn't been many kids to play with there, and he'd felt awkward at his new fancy private school. His father became totally immersed in the business; his mother got involved in her own projects. Doreen had dumped the auto mechanic's son and married blue-blooded Grant Tarrington. She'd been dazzled and impressed by her taste of high society.

Garek shook his head and glanced over at Ellie. She was wearing jeans and a sweater instead of an evening gown, but she sat as still and straight as she had at the symphony, listening to the music with every sign of pleasure.

Unlike Doreen, she never seemed impressed by wealth or status. He wondered how she'd gained such poise. She couldn't have had an easy life. In the last month he'd learned a lot about her family—how her mother's parents and siblings had come to this country from Mexico, and how they'd all worked hard to get jobs and educations.

Garek had heard all about Ellie's six cousins and their marriages and their offspring. He knew that her cousin Julio's six-year-old daughter had gotten an award at school for being "conscientious." He knew that her cousin Pedro's four-year-old son collected Pokémon cards.

But as much as Ellie talked about her cousins and their children, she rarely spoke of her mother and father.

The little he'd been able to glean was that her father had loved art and the violin, taken her to see symphony rehearsals when she was very small, and failed at just about every job he tried. Her mother had been kind and loving, but worn down by being virtually the sole support of the small family. And every summer she took Ellie on a bus to visit her family in Chicago.

Garek had guessed that her parents never married. That had been easy to deduce from the fact that she had her mother's last name and her reticence about her father's family. He also guessed that worry and uncertainty had shaped a large part of her early years.

He also guessed that the turmoil of her childhood was what had formed two of her most prominent characteristics: a love of her family and an ability to find enjoyment in even the most mundane activities and pastimes. She seemed to take pleasure in every aspect of her life.

Garek shifted on the hard folding chair. Perhaps that was the secret of her appeal. He didn't know what else it could be. Over the past four weeks he'd kept his word and hadn't tried to kiss her or touch her, even though sometimes it nearly killed him not to do so. He was aware of her all the time. At the art lecture they'd gone to last week, the chairs had been so close together that she'd brushed against him every time she moved. It had been extremely difficult to listen to the instructor.

He'd made an effort though, because he knew she would quiz him afterward. Professor Jameson had been exceedingly boring, but to Garek's surprise, the guest speaker had actually been interesting. The European woman had showed slides of her modern-art collection. She'd grown up with the Old Masters and loved them, but now preferred contemporary art because it was new and different and exciting. She'd talked about line and form, negative space and motion, color and connections. She'd showed how rational analysis could be applied to the way the art was structured, but also pointed out that logic could never explain the magic of the content contained within.

Garek had wanted to scoff at the woman's words, but somehow he couldn't. He'd been thinking of them when he went over to Doreen's the next night and offered to help Karen with her computer. The visit had been less than magical—Karen had been sullen and uncooperative—but Ellie had looked pleased when he told her about it.

"You can't expect miracles," she'd assured him. "Especially with a teenager."

"But why does she always seems so angry?"

"She's probably not very good at expressing her feelings. Or maybe she's just afraid to. Some kids have trouble with that."

"So you're saying I should just give up until she's an adult?"

"Adults can have the same problem." She gave him a pointed look, and he frowned, still not really understanding. She sighed. "Think of it like starting a business. You wouldn't work for one day and expect to make a million dollars, would you? You have to spend a lot of time and effort before it starts to pay off. A relationship is the same way."

Once again, her words stuck with him. He'd gone over to help Karen a second time—and had even stayed for dinner.

Doreen had been astonished.

The meal had been full of wary glances and awkward silences, but she'd invited him back the following week, and it had been easier that time. He'd been telling Karen about the time one of Doreen's boyfriends had come to the house to take her on a date. While Doreen was getting ready, Garek—still in junior high and barely five feet tall—had taken the brawny twenty-two-year-old Joe Pulaski into the living room and proceeded to ask him about his job, his income, whether he was planning to go to college, what his plans for the future were, and exactly how did Doreen fit into those plans? Joe, sweating and squirming, had leapt to his feet when Doreen came down, and rushed her out the door.

Karen had listened to the story expressionlessly, while Doreen sniffed and said what a little pest Garek had been...but then, unexpectedly, she'd smiled. And he'd smiled back. And then, suddenly, they'd both started laughing, and Karen, her mouth agape, had stared at them with wide, bewildered eyes—

A burst of applause interrupted Garek's thoughts. He glanced at Ellie, who was clapping vigorously. She had a way of explaining that made everything seem so clear and simple. But at the same time, when he was with her, he felt confused. Looking at her, he felt the same way he did when he looked at *Woman in Blue*. He could almost see it. Almost get it. Almost:…

The applause faded and everyone rose to their feet. Garek looked down at Ellie. Even with her heels on, the top of her head barely reached his chin. She was so small—and yet she was somehow becoming more and more important in his life.

"Will you let me take you to dinner?" he asked, raising his voice to be heard over the clanking scrape of metal chairs. She glanced over her shoulder, and he added with a smile, "Somewhere inexpensive, I promise."

For a moment, he saw an answering smile in her eyes. But then, just as quickly, it disappeared, and she turned away.

"I can't, I have other plans." She stepped into the aisle.

His smile vanished. Going after her, he caught her arm. "You have a date with someone else?"

"No…not exactly." She stared at the back of the man in front of her. "It's my cousin Alyssa's birthday. My aunt and uncle are having a party for her."

"I see."

Ellie shifted uneasily at the cool note in his voice. She'd thought about inviting him, but quickly decided against it. She couldn't imagine him with her family. They weren't rich. They were hardworking, respectable people, but she didn't know how he would react to them. A month ago, she would have thought he would look down his nose at them. Now, she wasn't quite so sure.

He'd surprised her these last few weeks. Now that the blinders were off, and she knew who and what he really was, she'd expected that spending time with Garek would banish any lingering feelings she had for him.

Instead, she'd noticed a change in him. He wasn't as

flip, as glib as he'd been before. He no longer seemed to be trying to charm her—but instead of liking him less, she actually liked him more. He no longer seemed as guarded, the remoteness she sometimes sensed in him seemed almost to have vanished. It only returned occasionally, like now. But this time, unlike before, she recognized what it meant—he was hurt.

The expression in his eyes bothered her more than she liked to admit, even to herself. He was trying really hard to establish a relationship with his sister and niece, but it was an uphill struggle. He seemed so...*alone* sometimes. As if he had no family at all.

But he probably liked it that way, she told herself. He would probably despise attending a fourteen-year-old's birthday party. It would only be a lot of silly games. And yet...she supposed it wouldn't hurt to ask him. He would probably say no. But at least she would have asked....

"Would you like to come with me?" she asked when they reached the entrance hall of the building and the crowd thinned out a little.

He stopped and stared at her, an expression that was hard to read in his eyes.

"You don't have to," she added hastily. "It would probably be embarrassing. Robbie will be there, and even though I made him promise not to tell anyone about what happened, he might let something slip—"

He pressed a finger to her lips. "I would be delighted to go."

He removed his finger immediately, but she was aware of a lingering tickle. Her lips felt dry, she wanted to lick them, but seeing how he was looking at her mouth, she didn't.

She wished she could stop remembering what it had felt like when he kissed her. She wished she could control the silly lurching of her stomach when he looked at her just so. She wished her heart didn't flutter happily to see the remoteness gone from his eyes.

She wished she'd kept her mouth shut.

And that feeling only intensified when they arrived at her aunt and uncle's and found Robbie out on the front porch, a beer in his hand.

He stood up, his eyes narrowing when he saw Garek. But then he smiled and slapped the other man on the back. "How's it going, *primo?*"

"He's not your cousin," Ellie said. "Remember what you promised me."

"Yeah, sure, Ellie. Come on inside, everyone else is already here."

Ellie relaxed a little. Everyone was going to be curious enough about Garek. The last thing she wanted was for them to find out about her silly "marriage"—

"Hey, everyone, look who's here," Robbie announced as they entered the crowded living room. "Ellie and her new husband!"

Several hours later, Ellie was exhausted. All evening she'd had to explain over and over that she and Garek *weren't* married, that it was just a joke on Robbie's part.

But in spite of her explanations, everyone still seemed to think Garek was her husband.

"I like your husband," Great-Grandma Pilar said at one point late in the evening. "He's a very nice young man. But you should have invited me to the wedding."

An image of Grandma Pilar—all four-foot-ten wizened inches of her—standing next to Caspar's tall, lanky frame as he intoned the ceremony popped into Ellie's head. Shuddering a little, she wondered how Grandma Pilar had formed any opinion at all of Garek since she spoke only Spanish. But she didn't ask. Instead, in the same language, she replied, "*Abuela*, he is *not* my husband."

But Grandma Pilar didn't seem to hear her. "A fine young man. He'll make fine babies. Are you pregnant yet?"

"No, Grandma," Ellie said resignedly.

"Better not wait," the old lady advised. "You're not getting any younger, you know."

Ellie muttered she was going to get something to eat.

Robbie was by the table, piling *carnitas* onto his plate. "I knew he was the one for you, Ellie. As soon as he punched me, I knew."

She might punch her cousin too if he didn't shut up. In desperation, she looked around for Garek.

He was dancing with Alyssa. Alyssa, all knees and elbows and braces, looked as though she was in seventh heaven—or maybe even eighth or ninth. Garek laughed at something the girl said, then, as if he felt her gaze on him, looked across the room straight at Ellie.

Their eyes met. He flashed a smile at her, then returned his attention to Alyssa, whirling her away in the dance.

Ellie inhaled sharply. She felt dizzy. She felt sick. In that split second, she knew the truth, the truth she'd been trying to deny.

She loved him.

In spite of everything, she loved Garek Wisnewski.

"I like your family," he said as he drove her home later that evening. "You're lucky to have a family like that."

"Yes, I know," she said. She did know it. But why did *he* have to recognize it, too? A ruthless businessman like him shouldn't have been able to see beyond the cramped house and poor clothes to the love and joy her family had. But obviously he had.

She stared out the window at the houses zipping by. She never should have agreed to keep going out with him. She was a thousand times a fool. But how could she have known her heart would be so treacherous?

He was arrogant and ruthless and bad-tempered. She'd thought she couldn't possibly fall in love with someone like that. But during the last few weeks she'd realized that his callous facade wasn't a true indication of his character. Rather, it was a form of protection. Against being hurt.

And he had been hurt. Not necessarily in large, traumatic ways, but in small, thoughtless ones. Not very many people had been kind to Garek Wisnewski. Whenever he talked about his parents, his sister or his ex-fiancée, there was a blankness to his expression. At first, she'd thought he just didn't care. But in the last few weeks, as he let his guard down more and more, she could sometimes see the pain in his eyes, the bewilderment. Sometimes she just wanted to put her arms around him and hold him as tightly as she possibly could.

He would be horrified if he knew what she was thinking. He would scoff at the idea that anyone had hurt him. In that respect he was a lot like his niece—both of them seemed determined to squash any and all emotions. Ellie suspected that to do so had become such a habit that they were now finding it difficult to recognize, let alone express their feelings. She doubted Garek would ever willingly talk about his feelings. Certainly he would never admit to something so sappy as love. He would never make himself so vulnerable.

Which meant that *she* was completely vulnerable.

They arrived at her apartment and he walked her to her door. "Thanks again for inviting me," he said, the dim porch light illuminating his face as he smiled down at her. "I'll pick you up tomorrow at noon."

"I...I can't see you tomorrow," she said, some sense of self-preservation belatedly kicking in.

He frowned. "Why not?" he asked bluntly, as incapable as ever of accepting a refusal graciously.

"Um, when I was talking to my uncle, he said he's shorthanded at the restaurant tomorrow and I told him I'd help out," she lied.

Garek's frown deepened. "Can't your uncle find someone else?"

"Everyone else is busy."

"That's not acceptable."

She stiffened. "What do you mean?"

"I mean, I don't want you working at the Taco Palace," he snapped.

"*You* don't want me to?" she snapped right back. "You have no right to tell me what to do."

"I'm your employer. I don't want you showing up at the gallery on Monday too exhausted to work."

"Oh, I should have known. You're worried about *business*. Heaven forbid I should botch a sale because I yawned in a customer's face. It's obvious you'll never change. I don't know why I ever thought you could." She crossed her arms across her chest, trying to protect herself against the wind. "Just go away."

"No. I want to talk to you."

"Well, I don't want to hear whatever it is you have to say."

His face was pale, his voice grim. "That's too bad, because you're going to have to listen."

"*Have* to?" she cried. "Why is that?"

"Because we're getting married—for real this time."

Chapter Fourteen

Ellie stared at him in astonishment. "Was that a proposal?"

"Yes."

His tight-lipped response was not exactly romantic. "It sounded like an order."

"Ellie…I…that is…oh, dammit." He closed his eyes and took a deep breath. When he opened them again, they looked a very dark green.

"I can't live without you, Ellie. Will you please marry me?"

The cold wind had stopped blowing at the beginning of his uncharacteristic, stammering speech. By the end, the clouds in the sky had parted and a moonbeam streamed down onto the porch. It danced over her skin and slipped inside her veins, making her feel as though she were lit from within. "Garek," she breathed. "Oh, Garek!" and hurled herself into his arms.

She saw the tension in his face disappear and an expression she'd never seen before light up his eyes, before his arms closed around her and he was kissing her fiercely.

She returned the kiss with equal strength, until she could barely breathe. She felt as though she were going to float up off the ground, her happiness was so intense.

With a choked laugh, he broke off the kiss. "I don't want to spoil your 'no sex before marriage' policy at this late date. Can you be ready tomorrow?"

She blinked up at him, surprised and rather disappointed. "Tomorrow?" she repeated vaguely, trying to resist the urge to unbutton his coat. "For what?"

"For our wedding, of course."

She gasped, his words dispelling her sensual haze, somewhat. "You want to get married tomorrow? That's impossible!"

His jaw tightened in that stubborn way she knew so well. "Why?"

A choked laugh escaped her. "I have to buy a dress, I have to give Martina time to find a new roommate, I have to get time off work—"

"I'll pay the rent for Martina and you can quit your job." His eyes dark and sensuous, he whispered, "I can't wait much longer, Ellie."

A shiver coursed through her. Of course, she wasn't going to quit her job or let him pay her rent. But the truth of the matter was, *she* didn't want to wait either. "Give me a week."

For a moment, she thought he was going to refuse. But then he said, "You've got your week—but I warn you—" his eyes gleamed "— I'm kidnapping you after that."

She laughed. "A week doesn't give me much time. I'm really going to have to cancel our date tomorrow."

"If you insist. But you'll have to make up for it now."

He kissed her—extremely thoroughly—until they were both breathing hard.

"Maybe it's better that I don't see you this week," he said huskily, resting his forehead against hers. "I can't take too much of this."

"Do we really have to wait?" she asked, still breathless. "Why don't you come inside?"

"Ellie…" He leaned back, his hand cupping the curve of her cheek, his gaze dark and serious. "For once in my life, I want to do the right thing. I'm going to marry you first."

She would have laughed at the grim determination in his voice if her throat wasn't suddenly so impossibly tight. "Oh, Garek," she whispered, blinking back foolish, happy tears.

He groaned. "Don't look at me like that, or I won't be able to help myself." He kissed her hard, then again, more slowly. "I can't go a whole week without seeing you. We can at least have lunch together. Monday. Come to my office around noon?"

She nodded. With one final kiss, he released her and thrust his hands into his pockets, as if to prevent himself from reaching out for her again. She went inside and closed the door, but couldn't resist running to the window to watch him go. He strode down the stairs to the sidewalk, looking tall and strong and handsome.

She hugged her arms around herself. She couldn't believe this was happening.

She supposed she shouldn't have said yes so quickly.

After all her doubts, after all their differences, she should have at least asked for some time to think it over.

But she hadn't been able to think. She'd been too surprised and too happy—too deliriously, ecstatically happy. She loved him. And he loved her.

She believed that with all her heart.

Whistling, Garek entered his office late Monday morning. Larry and Mrs. Grist were already there.

Garek smiled. "Good morning, Mrs. Grist, Larry," he said cheerfully.

Mrs. Grist responded civilly, but Larry only stared at him in astonishment.

"Mrs. Grist," Garek continued, ignoring Larry's silence, "would you please clear all appointments for two weeks—no, make that a month—starting next week. I will not be available."

Now Mrs. Grist looked startled. "But what about the meeting with the Lachland lawyers? They want to go over the independent auditor's report in detail. Most of the auditor's points are perfectly ridiculous, but the lawyers have a lot of questions—"

"Reschedule the meeting for this week," Garek said. "If they can't make it, suggest a teleconference."

Larry frowned. "What's happened?"

Garek looked at the two anxious faces before him. "Nothing," he said. "Except that Ellie and I are getting married."

An exclamation escaped Mrs. Grist. She beamed like a hundred lightbulbs. "Well, it's about time! Congratulations, Mr. Wisnewski. She's a fine young woman, and I'm sure you'll be very happy together."

Garek smiled back. "Thank you, Mrs. Grist." He glanced at Larry.

Larry, in contrast to Mrs. Grist, did not look at all pleased by Garek's news. In fact, he looked downright worried.

Garek arched an eyebrow. "Something wrong, Larry?"

"What? Oh, uh, no. Congratulations," Larry said hurriedly. "Uh, could I see you in your office?"

"Certainly." To Mrs. Grist, Garek said, "Ellie is coming to meet me for lunch. Have her come up immediately when she arrives."

In his office, Garek sat at his desk and looked at Larry's concerned face. "Yes?"

Larry hesitated a moment, then launched into speech. "This girl, Eleanor Hernandez—do you know anything about her finances?"

Garek arched a brow. "I haven't looked at her bank statement, no."

Larry's frown deepened. "I dislike having to be the voice of caution, but that is part of my job. You must get her to sign a prenuptial agreement."

Now it was Garek's turn to frown. "I hardly think that's necessary."

"It *is* necessary. You know as well as I do that fifty percent of all marriages end in divorce—"

"I have no intention of getting a divorce."

"No one does, Garek. But you've got to realize that people change, things go wrong, you can't always predict what your feelings will be five, ten, fifteen years from now."

"We're not getting divorced," Garek said, steel in his voice. "But even if we did, I would treat Ellie fairly."

"Yes, I'm sure you would. But her definition of fair

might be very different from yours. Believe me, after four divorces, I know what I'm talking about. Women can be very vindictive when they're angry."

"Ellie's not like that."

"Maybe not—but she would legally be entitled to a portion of all your assets—she might even try to go after your business. You owe it to your stockholders, if not yourself, to protect the company."

Garek frowned. As much as he hated to admit it, what Larry said made sense. He had a responsibility to the company. He couldn't shirk that just because he was getting married.

"How long will it take you to draft an agreement?" he asked abruptly.

"I'll have to consult with a prenuptial expert, get a financial statement from your accountant, write out a schedule of separate property and an expense-payment schedule and a waiver of interest in the business…although maybe it would be safer to establish a trust to protect Wisnewski Industries. I'm guessing a month, maybe two—"

"You have until Thursday."

"Until Thursday! But—" Larry stopped midsentence. Something in Garek's expression must have made him rethink what he was about to say.

"Very well," the lawyer agreed. "I'll have it ready."

Larry left, and Garek stared for a moment at the painting of *Woman in Blue*, before turning his gaze to the independent auditor's report on his desk. He could guess what it contained. Trouble. Lots of trouble.

The Lachland buyout had been progressing so smoothly—perhaps too smoothly. He damn well should have known that no deal ever happened that easily.

He picked up the phone.

"I'm going to have to spend the day going over the auditor's report," he told Mrs. Grist curtly. "Call Ms. Hernandez and cancel our lunch."

Chapter Fifteen

Ellie's treatment when she entered Wisnewski Industries on Thursday was very different from the first time she'd gone there. The security guard escorted her up the elevator himself, telling her that if she needed anything to just let him know.

"Thank you," Ellie responded, only half aware of his eager solicitude. She was thinking of Garek.

It was probably just as well that he'd canceled their lunch on Monday. She'd been terribly busy that whole day—and on Tuesday and Wednesday, also. She'd had to cancel her lease since Martina had decided to move in with friends who needed a third roommate. She'd also had to notify the utilities and the newspapers, both the *Tribune* and the *Sun Times*, and buy herself a wedding dress; she'd found a beautiful white lace frock in a small boutique off Michigan Avenue for half price. Ellie'd also arranged for Bertrice to fill in for her at the gallery while she was on her honeymoon. Bertrice had been reluctant at first, but had changed her mind when she heard how much Garek was paying.

The power of money, Ellie thought.

But the idea didn't bother her as much as it once had. She could put Garek's money to good use, she realized. She appreciated that now in a way she hadn't been able to a year ago. It had been silly of her to fear wealth. Money couldn't destroy what she and Garek had. She wouldn't let it.

But of course, that brought her to her other problem—there were a few things she should tell Garek. None of them was really relevant to their relationship, but he had a right to know.

She'd intended to tell him on Monday, but then his assistant had called to cancel. She hadn't thought too much about it, imagining that he must be extremely busy. She'd expected he would call her that night.

When he hadn't, she'd been half disappointed, half relieved. But then, when another day passed, and he still didn't call, she began to feel more and more uncertain.

Why didn't he call her? True, they'd agreed not to meet, but did that preclude telephone conversations, as well? Was he having second thoughts? Now that she thought about it, he hadn't really said he loved her. The words hadn't seemed necessary at the time. They'd been implicit in his actions.

Hadn't they?

Of course they had. She was acting like a ninny. She should just call him....

And so she had. He'd sounded a bit curt at first, but when she told him she wanted to meet him for lunch, he'd agreed.

"Tomorrow would be good. There's something I need to talk to you about," he'd said.

"Me, too." She hesitated a moment, then asked, "Is everything okay?"

"Yes." And then, "I just hate this damn waiting."

The frustration and longing in his voice had sent her spirits soaring. She'd been smiling when she hung up the phone.

He did love her, she thought now as she stepped off the elevator. And she loved him….

His assistant, talking on the phone, smiled and motioned her toward the office. Ellie entered quietly and saw him sitting at his desk, his hair rumpled, his tie askew, his jacket straining across his shoulders as he bent over some papers.

Dear heaven, how she loved him. For a moment, the emotion almost overwhelmed her. She felt fluttery and elated and buoyant just looking at him. How could she have doubted it for a second?

"Hello, darling," she said, a smile trembling on her lips as she stepped forward.

He looked up. Something blazed in his eyes, but he didn't return her smile. He had a tense look about his mouth and jaw. She heard a low cough. Turning, she saw a short man in a tailored suit rising from a chair.

Garek stood also. "Ellie, this is Larry Larson, the company lawyer. He has something for you to sign."

"Something for me to sign?" Ellie repeated in confusion. "What is it?"

Garek met her puzzled gaze steadily.

"A prenuptial agreement," he said.

Garek watched Ellie as Larry explained the contract to her. She was very quiet. She'd barely said a word since he'd first told her about the prenuptial agreement. She sat in the chair across from him, her face very pale.

What was she thinking? He didn't know. Except for one stunned glance at him when he'd made his announcement, she hadn't looked at him. She looked hurt. She looked as though he'd done something unspeakable.

Dammit, he thought angrily. She had no right to look like that. No right at all. It was common sense to settle their financial matters before they married. It made no difference to their relationship. Couldn't she see that?

Larry finished his explanation. He flipped to the back page of the document and showed her the signature line. "You just need to sign here," he said, holding out his pen.

Ellie didn't take the pen. Instead, she rose to her feet and gathered up the pages.

"Is something wrong?" Larry asked.

"No, not at all," she said calmly. "I just want to take it home and read through it."

Larry frowned. "But I explained all of the clauses to you."

"Yes, I know. I still want to read them over on my own."

Garek frowned also. "Is there something you don't understand?"

"No, not really."

"Then there's no reason to delay signing," the lawyer said, his voice a trifle chilly.

Her voice was equally cool. "I disagree. You've explained to me the necessity for this. Your reasons were practical. But I must be practical, also. It's only common sense to read something before I sign it, perhaps have my lawyer look it over."

Larry gaped at her.

She gave Garek a slightly shaky smile. "Do you mind if we skip lunch? I'm not very hungry…" She turned and walked out of the room.

Garek went after her.

"Ellie," he said, catching her elbow in the hall outside Mrs. Grist's office. "Dammit, it doesn't have to be like this—"

"Like what?"

Her expression was cool and remote—except for her eyes—her eyes were big blue pools of pain. Releasing her, he shoved his hands in his pockets and stepped back. "I can't take chances with the business."

"I know. I'm not mad, honestly. It's just that…oh, why does money have to ruin everything? Why does it make everything corrupt and ugly?"

He frowned at her. "You're exaggerating."

"I know. I know. I guess I'm still in shock. I wish you'd told me about this sooner."

"I've been busy." It was difficult suddenly to meet her gaze. "I just signed the Lachland buyout this morning. It means a lot to Wisnewski Industries."

"Does it? I'm happy for you, then." She turned her face away, brushing the dampness from her cheeks. "I'm sorry. I have to go." She hurried out the door.

"Ellie…" He started after her again, but a hand on his arm stopped him.

It was Larry.

"Let her go," the lawyer said. "Don't fall for the tears."

Garek glared at him. "What the hell are you talking about?"

"The tears." Larry shook his head. "Men fall for it every time. I fell for it four times myself. Leave her alone—she'll sign the prenup and she'll forget about it, believe me. Until the divorce. Um, *if* there's a divorce," he added hastily.

"Get the hell out of here," Garek snarled.

Larry beat a hasty retreat.

For the next several hours, Garek tried to concentrate on his work. He had plans to make now that the Lachland buyout had taken place. He could easily spend the next six months working out all the details. This was an exciting, challenging time for Wisnewski Industries. He should have had no trouble focusing on his work.

But then, he'd never been in a situation like this before.

He pushed away the profit-and-loss statements he was studying and leaned back in his chair. He wanted to marry Ellie. He'd made the decision impulsively, but he'd thought it was the right one. Only now he wasn't so sure.

Ever since Larry had brought up the subject of the prenuptial agreement, needles of doubt had poked at him. This whole marriage thing was more difficult than he'd thought it would be. He didn't like having demands put on him. And in her own way, he realized suddenly, Ellie was more demanding than Doreen and Amber combined.

He almost wished she did want money—that would have been easy to give. But Ellie wanted something more complicated than that.

He wished he'd just slept with her.

Only somehow, that wasn't enough. He wanted more, also. He wanted…what exactly? He didn't know. What the hell was the matter with him?

He frowned at the painting on the wall across from him.

Woman in Blue.

He'd disliked it at first. He'd thought it was silly and stupid and pointless. But somehow, over the last few months, it had begun to grow on him. It brightened up his office, made the room seem less dull, less enclosed. It was like having a window into an alternate reality.

As he looked at it now, he saw how the colors moved in sinuous tendrils and rhythmic scalloped patterns and how the blue became more and more intense as it moved toward the center of the painting. There was no one spot where you could see a change in hue, but the blue slowly, gradually, became brighter and brighter until in the very center it was an intense, bright sapphire….

And suddenly he understood.

Garek tried all afternoon and all evening to reach Ellie, but she seemed to have disappeared from the city of Chicago. Her phone had been disconnected and when he went to her apartment, the windows were dark and no one answered the door. He went to the gallery, but the idiot girl there said Ellie was on vacation. He even went to her aunt and uncle's house, but they only looked at him coolly and said they had no idea where she was.

The coolness made him think they were lying, that they knew something. He parked at the end of the street and lurked there for several hours, but there was no sign of Ellie.

He drove back over to her apartment and waited…and waited. Finally, at 3:00 a.m., he pounded on the door of the downstairs flat where Ellie's landlord lived, and convinced the man to unlock her door in case she was hurt.

Squinting in the glare from the kitchen lights, Garek looked at the bare walls, the packed suitcases.

"She said you two were getting married tomorrow," the landlord said. "You think she's changed her mind?"

Garek's gut twisted, squeezing the air out of his lungs and making it difficult to breathe. "No," he said more sharply than he'd intended.

"Uh-huh." The landlord looked pityingly at him.

Garek felt a sudden, strange sense of disorientation. The cramped, dark apartment faded from his consciousness, replaced by a memory of a different place—a brightly lit place with stark white walls. He'd been standing outside the hospital emergency room where the surgeons were operating on his father, waiting for someone to come out and tell him what was going on. The minutes had ticked by, turning with agonizing slowness into hours. He'd alternated between trying to calm his mother's and sister's hysterical crying, assuring them over and over again that the hospital had the city's finest doctors, that everything would turn out all right. They'd both finally fallen asleep on the couches in the waiting room. So he'd been the only one to see the expression in the doctor's eyes when he'd come in to talk to them—an expression very similar to the one in Ellie's landlord's eyes.

"No," Garek said again.

But this time his voice emerged a harsh, cracked whisper.

"I always thought he was a jerk," Robbie growled. "You should have let me smash his face that first time—"

"Robbie!" Ellie shifted on the dingy couch in his apartment. Her back still ached from sleeping on its springless cushions and she had a headache from Robbie's cologne, which he had a tendency to apply too heavily. She was in no mood to listen to his threats. "I need advice, not violence. I need logic and common sense."

"And you came to me?" Robbie, sitting on the couch next to her, dumped some more salsa on the cold taco he was eating for breakfast. A diced tomato flew into the air and landed on the prenuptial agreement lying on the coffee table next to his plate. "Hmm, well…" He grimaced. "You need to talk to your grandfather. He would know about this kind of stuff."

"No." Ellie brushed the tomato off the document and frowned at the slight red stain left on the paper. "I can handle this myself."

"But you can't," Robbie pointed out with impeccable logic. "Otherwise, you wouldn't have asked me for advice."

Ellie glared at him while he chomped on his taco. Yesterday, she'd just wanted a place where she could think without having to explain everything. But this morning, she wanted to talk about it—she wanted advice.

"You know, Ellie," Robbie said, swallowing a large bite, "I don't think you can really blame the guy for trying to protect his company."

"I don't. Not exactly. It's just…" She paused, struggling to put her feelings into words.

"It's just what?" Robbie asked.

"It's just that Garek has obviously put a lot of thought and time and consideration into his company." She swallowed the sudden lump in her throat. "I just wish he'd spare the same thought and time and consideration for me."

Robbie sighed. "Look, if the guy doesn't love you, he's an idiot and you should dump him."

"I think he does love me. I just don't think he knows *how* to love me."

"He's a virgin?" Robbie glanced down at his limp taco. "Well, if you want me to give him a few pointers—"

"No, that's not what I mean," Ellie said. "I mean he doesn't know how to have a relationship. I don't think he knows how to discuss things, how to compromise, how to allow himself to be vulnerable."

A doubtful look crossed Robbie's face. "Does any guy know how to do those things?"

"Maybe not." Ellie felt a burning behind her eyes. The sad thing was that she suspected that if Garek ever let down his guard, he would be more than capable of all those things—and much, much more. But it would take a long time for her to breach the walls he'd erected around himself. If she were lucky, in five or ten years, maybe—maybe—he would actually admit that he loved her.

Was she just wasting her time?

That's what she needed to know.

She never should have come to Robbie. She should have called Martina. Or Aunt Alma. Robbie was hopeless when it came to advice. He'd never had the least bit of common sense. He never let logic, or anything else, get in the way of his feelings.

But then again, maybe that was exactly the answer she was looking for.

Chapter Sixteen

Garek sat at his desk, staring bleary-eyed at the paper in front of him, the words running together in an unintelligible mess. He'd been trying to read it for the last hour, but his aching eyes and pounding head refused to cooperate. It was almost four o'clock in the afternoon and he still hadn't heard from Ellie. He'd told Mrs. Grist not to put any call through unless it was from her. So far, the phone had been completely silent.

He yanked at his tie, then pulled it off completely. He rose to his feet and paced around the room, rubbing his unshaven jaw. He'd left a note at her apartment. "You don't have to sign anything," he'd scrawled hastily. "Call me." Her landlord had promised to give it to her when she came back for her suitcases.

Garek had gone home after that, but he hadn't been able to sleep, so he'd come to the office. He had plenty of work to do.

Only, he hadn't done any of it.

He paced back to his desk, picked up the phone and dialed a number.

"Hello?" a slightly accented voice said.

"Mrs. Hernandez, this is Garek Wisnewski," he said. "Have you heard from Ellie?"

There was a slight pause. "In the fifteen minutes since you last called? No," she said.

"Will you please call me if she contacts you?"

"Yes, I will," she said, her voice a mixture of sympathy and impatience. "Goodbye, Mr. Wisnewski."

He sat back down, resting his head on his hands. The same fear he'd felt last night standing in her apartment was twisting his gut again, only more tightly, more viciously than before.

Had he lost her?

An image floated in his head, a vision of how she'd looked the day before, her face pale, her eyes wide and dark with hurt.

He squeezed his tired, burning eyes shut, trying to banish the picture. He hadn't meant to hurt her. He never should have given her that prenuptial agreement. He was an idiot. If she would just come back, he would apologize, tell her what a fool he'd been. He would make it up to her....

If he ever got the chance.

Why didn't she call?

Maybe something had happened to her. What if she'd been in an accident? What if she'd been mugged and her purse snatched? She was a fool for going around the city in that damn train at all hours of the day and night. What if she was in the hospital right now, critically injured, with no identification, unable to speak—

He jumped to his feet, picked up the phone and buzzed Mrs. Grist.

"Mr. Wisnewski!" her voice came on the line. "I was just about to ring you—"

"Has she called?" Hope flared in his chest.

"No, but Mr. Larson wants to talk to you—"

Hope turned to ashes. "Tell Larry to go to hell," he growled. "I want you to call the local hospitals. See if anyone answering to Ellie's description has been admitted in the last twenty-four hours—"

"Yes, Mr. Wisnewski, but—"

"No buts. Call the police, too. See if there've been any accidents—"

"But Mr. Larson said it was about Ellie—"

"And have security see what they…Ellie? What about Ellie?"

"I don't know exactly. He just said you need to come down to the conference room. He said it's important."

Garek frowned. Had Larry found out something? Was Ellie *here?*

He hurried down to the second floor, but when he entered the conference room, there was no sign of Ellie—just a phalanx of gray-suited, black-briefcased businessmen. They looked like robots—except for the short, red-faced man in a green plaid suit at one end of the table.

The man looked familiar, although it took Garek a moment to place him—Calvin G. Hibbert, financier and wealthy scion of the blue-blooded Hibbert family. One of his companies had been competing with Wisnewski Industries for the Lachland Company. What the hell was he doing here?

"Ah, Garek, there you are!" Larry's usually neatly

combed hair was disheveled, the bald spot in plain view. In an undertone, he added, "You are not going to *believe* what's happening—"

"Mr. Garek Wisnewski?" One of the robotic clones spoke when he heard Garek's name. "I am Rex Rathskeller, senior partner of the firm Rathskeller, Broad and Campbell. These gentlemen are Mr. Broad, Mr. Campbell and our associates, Mr. Pesner, Mr. White and Mr. Kiphuth."

Garek frowned. He'd heard of the firm. Headquartered in Philadelphia, it was considered one of the best in the nation. "If this has something to do with Lachland—"

"Lachland?" The lawyer appeared confused until one of his colleagues whispered in his ear. His forehead cleared. "Ah, I see. No, Mr. Wisnewski, this has nothing to do with your company's business. No, we've been hired by our client to discuss a prenuptial agreement—"

A ringing sounded in Garek's ears, obscuring the rest of the man's sentence. He'd spent the last twenty-four hours rushing all over the city looking for Ellie, half out of his mind with fear and worry—and she'd been off hiring a pack of lawyers? And not just any lawyers. She'd hired the most experienced, most cutthroat, most *expensive* lawyers in the business. She'd certainly changed her tune—

Larry's frantic voice penetrated the haze. "Mr. Rathskeller claims that Ellie isn't penniless. He claims that she has money of her own. He claims that—"

"He doesn't claim anything," the old man in green announced coldly. "He states facts. I am Calvin G. Hibbert, and Eleanor Graciela Hibbert Hernandez is my granddaughter. And she possesses a trust fund in excess of two hundred million dollars—"

Larry's eyes bugged out. "Two…hundred…million…!" he gasped, sinking into a chair.

For a moment, no one spoke, the silence broken only by Larry's choking noises.

Then, suddenly, the door to the conference room swung open.

A small woman with tousled black curls and large blue eyes peered in. For a moment, she appeared startled by all the men in the room. Then she saw Hibbert.

"Grandpa?" she gasped. And then, "Grandpa!"

Suddenly, she ran to the head of the table and threw herself into his arms, laughing and hugging and kissing him. "Grandpa, what on earth are you doing here?"

Chapter Seventeen

Garek's immediate reaction upon seeing her had been relief that she was all right. But before the relief could even sink in, she'd flown into the old man's arms, hugging and kissing him. Garek clenched his teeth. Not only had she *lied* to him…she hadn't even *noticed* he was in the room.

All her attention was wrapped up in the old man. Calvin G. Hibbert. One of the wealthiest men in the country. Her *grandfather*.

"Your cousin Robert called me," Hibbert was explaining. "The first time in his life that young man ever showed any common sense, I'm sure. *He* told me that my only granddaughter was getting married."

Ellie blushed guiltily. "I'm sorry, Grandpa. I wasn't sure—"

"I came straightaway," he said, waving away her faltering explanation and casting a disparaging glance at

Garek. "I wanted to meet this fiancé of yours. I must say, Eleanor, I don't think much of your choice—"

"Grandpa—"

"But Robert says he's better than the last one. At least he appears to have a little bit of his own money. I don't like the sound of this prenuptial agreement, though. I don't want you to get cheated out of your inheritance."

"What inheritance?" Her smile faded and her tone grew cool. "You disowned me, remember?"

It was Hibbert's turn to blush, the hue of his skin changing from red to scarlet. "Nonsense," he blustered. "You know I didn't mean it. I was just angry."

"You meant it when you disowned my father."

"Well, harrumph, I learn from my mistakes." His voice turned gruff. "You're all I have, Eleanor."

Her eyes grew misty. "Oh, Grandpa…"

"Ms. *Hibbert,* I hate to interrupt this touching reunion," a sarcastic voice intruded. "But may I speak to you a moment? Alone."

Ellie glanced up to see Garek holding the door open to a small adjoining office. Black bristles stood out on his tightly clenched jaw. His eyes were narrow red slits.

Uh-oh.

She walked the length of the room, conscious of the roomful of lawyers watching her, and into the office. Garek closed the door and leaned back against it, his arms folded across his chest.

"Well?" he demanded.

She glanced at him uncertainly. "What happened to you? You look awful—"

"Don't try to change the subject…*Eleanor.*"

She looked down to where her fingers were twisting the strap of her purse. "I suppose I should have told you—"

"You *suppose?* Exactly when were you going to tell me that you had *two hundred million dollars* sitting in the bank?"

"It wasn't like that. My grandfather and I had a fight when I moved out. I haven't even seen or talked to him in over a year. I didn't want to be controlled by him and his money anymore. He disowned me, and that was fine with me."

"He doesn't appear to consider you disowned."

"Apparently he changed his mind."

"You must have known that was likely."

"Actually, it seemed highly *un*likely. He did the same thing to my father. My parents lived in poverty because Grandpa disapproved of his son's marriage to a Mexican house cleaner. It wasn't until my mother and father died that he took me in. And he soon let me know who was in control. He picked my school, my friends, even the men I dated. When I couldn't stand it anymore, I moved out."

"That really doesn't explain why you didn't tell me about all this."

She darted a quick glance at him. "Sometimes people act…differently toward me when they know how much my grandfather is worth."

"I see. So I had to believe that you loved me for myself and not my money, but you weren't willing to extend the same trust to me?"

"It wasn't like that! It didn't seem important. Especially since Grandfather had disowned me. I would have been perfectly happy if it were true. Money spoils everything."

"That's bull." Garek took a step forward. "Everyone has to have money to survive. You just want to live in a fairy-tale world where you can pretend money doesn't exist, where you don't have to accept responsibility for your own survival. Money makes everything better."

"Not everything," she said quietly.

"Get over it," he said curtly. "So maybe your grandfather tried to control you—there's lots worse problems—like not having enough food to eat, not having a home."

She nodded slowly, remembering her father's futile efforts to hold on to a job and how tired her mother had been coming home after cleaning houses all day. "I know I shouldn't complain…but it's not just the control. When I moved in with my grandfather, everyone treated me differently. People who never would have given me the time of day suddenly sought me out. Everyone laughed at every stupid joke I told. Men told me I was the most beautiful, exciting, wonderful woman ever to walk the earth. I never knew for sure who really meant what they said."

Garek opened his mouth to dismiss her excuse, then paused. Actually, what she said had some truth in it. He'd experienced it himself.

"Rafe told me he loved me, but he couldn't dump me fast enough when my grandfather disinherited me," she continued, not noticing his distraction. "People *think* about me differently, knowing I have all that money. *You* probably think of me differently."

Again, he started to deny it, then paused, realizing that it was true. In a few, fundamental ways, their relationship had completely changed. No longer was he the wealthy businessman rescuing the poor working girl from a life of poverty. In some way that he hadn't even recognized until now, his money had given him an advantage over her. A sense of superiority, perhaps, a sense that she should be *grateful* to him.

His financial status no longer gave him that edge over her—in fact, the exact opposite was true. *She* had more money than *he* did. The thought wasn't pleasant.

Frowning, he looked at her. "I suppose it does change things—"

She stepped back, a stricken look coming over her face. "I understand—"

He reached out and grabbed her arm. "No, you don't, Ellie. I can't deny that it changes how people will look at us. But it *doesn't* change how I feel about you."

She looked at him. "And exactly how do you feel about me, Garek?"

He let go of her arm. He stood silently, not speaking. Ellie felt as though her heart was cracking in two. She turned again to leave, but then he spoke, his voice quiet.

"That painting," he said. *"Woman in Blue."*

She stopped in her tracks.

"I didn't like it at first. It made no sense, the colors and shapes seemed haphazard and inexplicable. But when I looked harder, I noticed a balance in the picture, an equilibrium that somehow connected all the elements together. And then I noticed how intense the blue was. How bright. How true."

She felt him standing behind her. "It's you, isn't it, Ellie? *Woman in Blue* is you. It took me a long time to figure it out, but I finally did. And that's when everything became clear."

He took her shoulders and turned her to face him. "I've made a lot of stupid mistakes, Ellie, like asking you to sign that prenuptial agreement. You gave me a second chance once, and now I'm having to ask you for a third one. This relationship business is a lot harder than I realized. But I'm willing to learn. I'm a hard worker and I'll do whatever it takes to make our relationship work because I love you, Ellie. I love you, and if you'll marry me, I'll spend the rest of my life proving it to you."

"Oh, Garek." She smiled shakily. "I love you so much."

And then, suddenly, she was in his arms and he was kissing her as if she was more valuable, more beautiful, more precious than a museum full of the finest art in the world.

"Oh, Garek," she sighed again when they finally had to come up for oxygen. Her cheeks stung from the scrape of his whiskers, but she was too happy to care. "Let's give the lawyers the prenuptial agreement and go."

He brushed a curl back from her forehead, his fingers lingering on her skin. "What prenuptial agreement?"

"The one Larry prepared. When I really thought about it, I realized that I've let money control me. I believed money was causing all my problems. But it was me and my own fear causing the problems, not the money. I knew I loved you too much to let anything spoil what we had. I have the contract right here, all signed." She pulled the sheaf of papers out of her purse.

He looked at the documents, then at her. "You signed it even after I told you not to?"

She stared at him. "You told me not to sign it?"

"In the note I left with your landlord this morning." His forehead creased. "Didn't you read it?"

"I haven't been home." She looked up at him, touched beyond words that he'd trusted her enough to tell her not to sign the agreement. "But it really doesn't matter now. Let's give it to the lawyers."

He frowned. "That's not going to work. We need a new prenuptial agreement."

Her smile faltered. "But why?"

"To protect your inheritance."

"I trust you."

"I know you do." He looked down into her troubled eyes. "It's only practical," he said gently.

"It just seems so sordid," she sighed.

He stared at her thoughtfully. "Why don't we let the lawyers hash out the money issues and we come up with our own agreement."

"Our own agreement?" Frowning, she watched him pull a pen and paper out of a drawer and motion her to sit down at the desk. She sat down uncertainly. "What do you mean?"

"I mean—write this down—you must never take me to a lecture by Professor Jameson again."

A smile began to curve her lips. Obediently, she wrote down, *Eleanor G. Hibbert Hernandez promises never to take Garek Wisnewski to a Jameson lecture.* She then went on to write:

Eleanor G. Hibbert Hernandez gets to choose all the art for the house.

"Hmm." He pretended to consider that one. "Very well—as long as you don't buy anything from Caspar."

She glanced up at him, smiling. "Not even for the bathroom?"

"Especially not for the bathroom. I want that in writing."

Laughing, she complied. "Very well…but we have to spend Christmas Eve at my family's."

"No argument from me there." He paused a moment, then added slowly, "I'd like to invite my sister and niece, though."

She smiled at him. "That's a good idea."

He grimaced a little. "I'm not so sure. I may live to regret it."

"No, you won't," she said firmly.

He looked at her, a smile quirking the corners of his mouth. "I believe you. Speaking of holidays, that reminds me... You must never buy me a tie again."

"I thought you liked the tie I gave you."

"I do," he said firmly. "I like it so much I want it to forever be unique in my closet."

"But I could find something different—"

"No."

She pouted a little. "All right. But you can't buy me any jewelry then."

He crouched beside her and looked into her eyes. "I'm afraid I already broke that one." He pulled a small box out of his pocket and handed it to her. "Open it, Ellie."

With trembling fingers, she lifted the lid. Her breath caught. A simple platinum ring with a small, exquisitely cut sapphire. "Oh, Garek, it's beautiful." She looked up at him, tears in her eyes. "Maybe I'll make an exception—just this once."

He pulled her out of the chair and kissed her.

A while later, they came out of the office into the conference room and headed for the door.

Hibbert watched as the couple, smiling at each other, strolled toward the door. He frowned. "Where are you two going?"

"To the courthouse," Ellie replied. "To get married."

"B-b-but what about the prenuptial agreement?" Larry sputtered.

"Ellie and I have written up our own arrangement."

Garek looked at the roomful of lawyers. "You have this afternoon to come up with an agreement acceptable to both sides. Otherwise, you're all fired."

Without another word, Garek and Ellie strolled out of the room.

"This afternoon!" Mr. Rathskeller exclaimed. "That's impossible."

Hibbert, who was still staring after the couple thoughtfully, turned his eaglelike gaze on the lawyer. "Nothing's impossible. Write up something fair and equitable. That's all you have to do. But you'd better get to it instead of sitting around bellyaching."

The lawyers grumbled as they opened their briefcases and pulled out sheaves of paper.

"Love," one of them muttered in disgust.

Hibbert moving over to stand by the window, frowned deeply, his eyebrows beetling. He was about to make a comment, when he saw Garek and Eleanor come out of the front door of the building. Apparently too impatient to wait for the limo, Garek hailed a taxi and the couple climbed in. As they drove away, through the rear window Hibbert could see the two of them kissing.

The corner of his mouth lifted.

"Yes," he murmured, sounding wistful. "Love."

* * * * *

MILLS & BOON

Live the emotion

Modern
romance™

THE ITALIAN'S FUTURE BRIDE by *Michelle Reid*

Rafaelle Villani was used to loving and leaving women. Then a newspaper photo mistakenly suggested he had finally been harnessed…by innocent Rachel Carmichael. Rafaelle lost no time in claiming his fake fiancée. But soon Rachel feared she had conceived his baby…

PLEASURED IN THE BILLIONAIRE'S BED
by *Miranda Lee*

Lisa was the ultimate ice princess – she didn't do casual flings, especially not with rich playboys like Jack Cassidy! But it took just one long, hot night to unleash the desire Lisa had never dared submit to – and the realisation she might be pregnant…

BLACKMAILED BY DIAMONDS, BOUND BY MARRIAGE by *Sarah Morgan*

The Brandizi Diamond came into the possession of the Kyriacou family generations ago. When Nikos Kyriacou discovers Angelina Littlewood has the jewel, he must get it back. But does Angie have her own reasons for wanting to keep it?

THE GREEK BOSS'S BRIDE by *Chantelle Shaw*

Kezia Trevellyn is in love with her boss, Greek tycoon Nik Niarchou. When she accompanies Nik on a luxury cruise, Kezia's dreams become reality and a powerful affair erupts. Kezia almost forgets the one secret reason why their relationship can't last – until Nik proposes…

On sale 5th January 2007

Available at WHSmith, Tesco, ASDA, Borders, Eason, Sainsbury's and most bookshops

www.millsandboon.co.uk

From No. 1 *New York Times* bestselling author Nora Roberts

Two tales of love found at Christmas featuring

Home for Christmas

and

All I Want for Christmas

On sale 1st December 2006

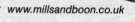

FREE!

4 Books
and a surprise gift!

We would like to take this opportunity to thank you for reading this Mills & Boon® book by offering you the chance to take FOUR more specially selected titles from the Modern Romance™ series absolutely FREE! We're also making this offer to introduce you to the benefits of the Mills & Boon® Reader Service™—

- ★ FREE home delivery
- ★ FREE gifts and competitions
- ★ FREE monthly Newsletter
- ★ Exclusive Reader Service offers
- ★ Books available before they're in the shops

Accepting these FREE books and gift places you under no obligation to buy, you may cancel at any time, even after receiving your free shipment. Simply complete your details below and return the entire page to the address below. You don't even need a stamp!

YES! Please send me 4 free Modern Romance books and a surprise gift. I understand that unless you hear from me, I will receive 6 superb new titles every month for just £2.80 each, postage and packing free. I am under no obligation to purchase any books and may cancel my subscription at any time. The free books and gift will be mine to keep in any case.

P6ZEF

Ms/Mrs/Miss/Mr ....Initials................................
BLOCK CAPITALS PLEASE
Surname ....
Address..

....

....Postcode ....

Send this whole page to:
UK: FREEPOST CN81, Croydon, CR9 3WZ

Offer valid in UK only and is not available to current Mills & Boon® Reader Service™ subscribers to this series. Overseas and Eire please write for details. We reserve the right to refuse an application and applicants must be aged 18 years or over. Only one application per household. Terms and prices subject to change without notice. Offer expires 28th February 2007. As a result of this application, you may receive offers from Harlequin Mills & Boon and other carefully selected companies. If you would prefer not to share in this opportunity please write to The Data Manager, PO Box 676, Richmond, TW9 1WU.

Mills & Boon® is a registered trademark owned by Harlequin Mills & Boon Limited.
Modern Romance™ is being used as a trademark. The Mills & Boon® Reader Service™ is being used as a trademark.